In the Time of Dinosaurs

PART II

Look for other **ANIMORPHS**® titles by K.A. Applegate:

the andalite chronicles

ANIMORPHS®
\<MEGAMORPHS #2\>

In the Time of Dinosaurs PART II

K.A. Applegate

AN
APPLE
PAPERBACK

SCHOLASTIC INC.
New York Toronto London Auckland Sydney

Cover illustration by David B. Mattingly

ISBN 0-590-02358-6

Copyright © 1998 by Katherine Applegate.
All rights reserved. Published by Scholastic Inc.
ANIMORPHS, APPLE PAPERBACKS and logos are trademarks and/or registered trademarks of Scholastic Inc.

12 11 10 9 8 7 6 5 4 3 2 1   8 9/9 0 1 2 3/0

Printed in the U.S.A.   40

First Scholastic printing, June 1998

For Michael and Jake

In the Time of Dinosaurs

PART II

CHAPTER 1
Rachel

They were around me. All around me. Maybe ten of them. Deinonychus, Tobias had called them. Like wolves. They circled me like wolves.

They were not big, certainly smaller than my grizzly bear morph. Maybe ten feet from half-grinning mouth to rigid tail. But they were dangerous. Even with my dim grizzly bear eyesight, I could see their bristling weapons. The scythe-clawed hands; the huge ripping talon; the razor-sharp teeth.

I had weapons of my own. I had strength enough in my arms and shoulders to push over a Toyota. I had my own evil, ripping claws. I had teeth. But I was not fooled. I knew my only hope was that the Deinonychus would be discouraged by the fact that I was unknown prey.

Maybe the pack could be scared off. Maybe they wouldn't like the smell of bear. I wondered if Tobias was safe up in his tree. I hoped so.

The leader, the Deinonychus with the shortened tail, stepped to the front.

"HhhooorrRAAWWWRR!" I roared, and rose up erect to my impressive seven-plus feet. In my own time, there was no land predator as large or with as much raw power as a grizzly. But this was a whole different time. And a way, way different standard of large.

I knew these Deinonychus shared an environment with Tyrannosaurus and probably a dozen other very big, very dangerous lizards. And they thrived in that environment. How was I ever going to scare them?

The leader cocked his head and listened to me roar. He looked directly at me, considering, wondering.

Then two of them leaped!

"RROOAAARRR!" I bellowed. I swung my meat-hook claw with all my might. It was a lucky blow. I caught the closest Deinonychus across the neck. He collapsed.

With no signal that I could see, they all backed away. The leader sniffed at me. He sniffed at his comrade, who was no longer moving. Intelligent eyes considered.

This time I heard a signal. It was almost the cheeping of a songbird. "Neep!"

The Deinonychus pack circled around. It was so precise. So planned, almost rehearsed. They were not running away. They were not giving up. Instead they were preparing a more concerted attack.

They were prepared to take losses. That meant they would press the attack this time. Press the attack till I was down. Till I was food.

But something wasn't right. I could see it in the leader's eyes. He was glaring hard at a Deinonychus that had just arrived.

This new dinosaur stepped forward. He sniffed at me from a safe distance. And then, without warning, he leaped!

A slash with his left foot claw ripped a two-foot-long slice in my chest. It hadn't cut deep into vital organs but it hurt.

"HhhhRROOOAAARRR!" I bellowed.

But there was an even louder roar. The leader of the pack screamed at the impertinent new dinosaur. The new Deinonychus jumped back, away from me, and spun around to face the enraged pack leader.

The two Deinonychus stood bristling, face-to-

face. A challenge! That was it. The new Deinonychus had ignored the leader. He'd attacked on
his own. And that was an attack on the leader's
dominance.

The leader hissed. It was a low, sinister
sound. He stuck his tail straight back. The challenger raised his clawed hands, ready for battle.

And it was only then that I spotted the twisted
pieces of fabric around the challenger's arm.
Fabric torn from my own leotard and wrapped
around Tobias's splint.

<Tobias!> I cried. It *was* Tobias. It had to be.
But he had ripped a hole in me . . . .

I realized what had happened. Tobias had
somehow acquired this Deinonychus's DNA and
morphed him. But in doing so he'd lost control.
The Deinonychus's instincts had pushed Tobias's
mind aside and taken control.

And now Tobias was in a showdown with the
pack leader. A showdown to determine who
would be boss. And who would be in charge of
destroying me.

Tobias and the leader circled each other
slowly, warily.

<Tobias! Listen to me. You've morphed a di-
nosaur. You've lost control. It happens sometimes. You need to —>

The pack leader leaped! He landed, deadly
feet out, mouth snapping, right where Tobias had

been a split second before. But Tobias had dodged left, then crouched low to get in under the leader's guard.

Chomp!

"ScrrEEEEE!"

The leader jumped back, shocked. A piece of his left flank was missing.

Tobias circled again, tail stiff as a pole behind him.

Now the leader was more cautious. He waited for Tobias to make the first move. It wasn't a long wait. Tobias charged. With split-second timing, the other dinosaur jumped up in the air. He met Tobias's face with his own wicked talons.

Slash!

"ScrrrEEEE-uh!" Tobias fell back. Blood gushed from a wound in his face. The pack leader pressed the attack. Tobias stumbled back in seeming panic.

"Hrrooo-HAH!" A cry of triumph came from the pack leader. He leaped.

Too soon! Tobias was under him, ripping upward with his forepaws. He jammed his claws into the other Deinonychus's chest.

The pack leader screamed and flailed. But he could not tear Tobias's teeth away from him. It was over.

Tobias stood up. And he screeched a loud cry of challenge.

"Hreee-YAH! Hreee-hrEEEE-YAH!"

He looked at the rest of the pack. They looked at their fallen leader. Then they looked at Tobias. And one by one, like vanquished knights offering their swords to the victor, they each lowered their noses to the ground in submission.

Tobias turned. Turned to look at me.

<Tobias, it's me, Rachel. Listen to me, it's Rachel.>

I was using one paw to hold my own wound closed. The pain was intense. But the fear was greater. I saw the look in Tobias's eyes.

<Tobias, you are human. You are human. Get control of the morph!>

He advanced toward me. He was hungry. The others advanced just a step behind him.

<Tobias! Listen to me. You are a human be-ing! It's me, Rachel. Your friend. You are human, you . . .>

No, I realized. No, that was wrong, wasn't it?

<Tobias. You are a *hawk*. You are a red-tailed hawk. Remember your wings? Remember flying? Flying high on the thermals?>

His deadly jaw was inches away. He stopped. He tilted his head. And suddenly, his entire body seemed to shudder.

<Rachel?> he said.

CHAPTER 2

Jake

Down it came. Like having the Goodyear blimp dropped on top of you. Only much, much heavier.

I couldn't see a thing, only feel the air rush aside as the beast fell. I rolled.

WHUUUUUMP!

"Aaaahhh!" I cried. I was pinned. My legs were caught beneath the long-necked dinosaur's belly. Just my lower legs, and nothing had been broken, but when I tried to move I realized I was trapped.

"Jake!" Cassie cried. "Where are you?"

I wanted to tell her to shut up and save herself. Another part of me wanted to beg her to help me.

I was shaking. Literally shaking. Like I had fever chills and I just couldn't stop them.

CHOMP!

The huge head came down and ripped violently into the long-necked dinosaur.

CHOMP!

The Tyrannosaurus was eating ravenously. Just a couple of feet above my head. Then I guess it chomped into something tough, because it yanked. And that yanking lifted the big dinosaur's weight off me for a second.

I was out!

I rolled. I jumped to my feet.

"Ooof!" I went down. My legs had gone numb from being pinned. I could move them, but —

Down it came! Flashing teeth all around me. No way out. I curled into a ball.

"Oh, God!" I cried.

The Tyrannosaurus's jaw closed around me. I clenched my arms and legs tight together. Still those teeth cut grooves in my left shoulder. No room! The mouth was too narrow. I pushed my numb legs out before me, down the Tyrannosaurus's throat.

I was in the Tyrannosaurus's mouth. No room to move. Stinking foul air. Sticky saliva all over me. A big tongue that tried to push the rest of me down the waiting, greedy throat. He closed his mouth and crushed the air out of my lungs.

8

I grabbed that tongue. I locked my fingers on the rough, wet thing and focused with all that was left of my terrified, jibbering brain.

I wasn't even sure I'd acquired the DNA when I started trying to morph. I was doing it all at once. I was acquiring and morphing and screaming in terror.

But I began to grow. I couldn't be near those teeth when I grew. They would lacerate me. I wormed down the roaring Tyrannosaurus's throat. Down away from the teeth. Its powerful throat muscles were pummeling my legs now, but I was morphing.

The Tyrannosaurus realized something was wrong. It had swallowed the wrong thing. It coughed and gacked. Then, a massive surge of muscle spasm, and I was falling.

Flump!

I hit the soft side of the fallen long-necked dinosaur. I tried to grab on, but failed. My hands weren't my hands anymore.

I rolled onto the ground at the Tyrannosaurus's feet. I was at his mercy. Utterly.

But the big monster was not able to attack. Something had happened to its insides. I don't know if I ruptured something, or what. But the tyrant lizard stomped three, four, five steps away and collapsed. It sat down on its tail, then fell over onto its side, moaning.

I lay there gasping, not knowing what body I had, not caring. I was alive. I tried my mouth. No, I couldn't talk. I demorphed. Then tried again.

"Cassie! Marco! Ax!"

"Jake?" Cassie's voice cried in the darkness.

It took a few seconds for us to find each other back at the glowing embers of the campfire. Cassie put her arms around me, slime and all, and hugged me. I was too shaky to return the hug, but it felt good.

"Is it dead?" Marco asked.

"No," I said. "But I think I hurt it. It's on its side over there, I think."

"You know what we should do," Marco said grimly. "We should all acquire that Tyrannosaurus. We need one alive to acquire. It's alive. Until we acquire a Big Rex we're just going to get chased around till sooner or later we get eaten."

"I already did it," I said. "But you're right."

None of them were anxious to walk over and start touching that creature. Even moaning on its side, it was terrifying.

We came up slowly, carefully, tentatively beneath the tail. We carried small torches to light our way.

Marco was the first. He pressed his hand against the crocodilelike flesh.

And then Ax.

And lastly Cassie.

It was strange. Like some kind of ritual. Three humans and an alien, all carrying torches that might as well have been cinders in the endless darkness. We cowered before the groaning, wheezing monster and touched it.

"It's so strange," Cassie said. "We're humans in a time millions of years before the first humans. In our time, Homo sapiens run the planet. In this time it's the Tyrannosaurus. You always wonder who would have won, if humans and dinosaurs had lived at the same time. Who would have survived?"

"They would have hunted us like cats hunt mice," Marco said. "Primitive humans with sharp sticks and maybe a couple of torches? No contest."

<Yes, but you are not just *primitive* humans,> Ax said. <You are primitive humans with Andalite morphing technology.>

Not for the first time, I wondered if Ax had developed a sense of humor.

And then the adrenalin and lack of sleep and the physical beating all came together. My eyes closed all on their own. My legs buckled. I fell, and arms reached out to take me.

CHAPTER 3

Marco

 fter we let Jake sort of doze for awhile, we decided that maybe sleeping between a dead long-necked dinosaur the size of Nebraska and a moaning, sick Tyrannosaurus was not a great idea.

So despite the fact that it was so dark we couldn't see our own feet, we trudged on. At least it wasn't raining. After that big huge flash, I'd assumed rain was coming. But maybe that's not the way it worked in this millennium.

"So basically everything is fine," I said, shifting my pathetically dim torch to my other hand. "We're tens of millions of years in the past. We have no food except charred scraps of dinosaur-on-a-stick. There's a river over there, but if we do go and get a drink, some monster crocodile will jump out and chomp us. We're lost, which is fine because let's face it, we're not exactly looking for the nearest Taco Bell, so who cares where we are? Plus, just to make things perfect, we're wearing Tyrannosaurus skin sandals, which is going to really, really endear us to the next Big Rex we see."

"I wish Rachel were here," Cassie said.

"Yeah," I said, suddenly sad. "She'd say something like, 'I can stand the dinosaurs, Marco, I just can't stand listening to you whine.'"

Jake laughed softly. "You do a pretty good Rachel impression."

I heard Cassie sniffle.

"You know what occurs to me," I said. "We survived, right? I mean, twice we've been jumped by tyrannosaurs or tyrannosauri, whichever. I'm still here and I'm not Captain Heroic. And Jake is still here, despite the fact he's a big, galumphing, clumsy oaf, and not even all that bright."

"Thanks," Jake said.

"My point is, if *we* could survive, are you going to tell me Rachel and Tobias — Xena, Warrior Princess, and a Bird-boy who has to hunt his breakfast every morning — *didn't* make it? Come on, anything that wants to kill Rachel would have to be meaner than Rachel. And you know that's not even possible."

Cassie chuckled. She sniffled, too. The truth

was I was talking total bull, but who knew? Maybe somehow Rachel and Tobias really did make it. It was easier to believe they did.

I've always said you make a choice in this world. You can see the world as being tragic, or you can see it as being funny. Some things just flat-out aren't funny, of course. But with very few exceptions, you can usually find the humor in life and in people. I guess if you want to see the world as being sad, terrible, unfair, boo-hoo boo-hoo, that's fine. But man, what kind of life is that?

We trudged. We stopped and dozed. We got up and trudged some more. And gradually that humongous comet in the sky grew faint as the sky began to light up with the rising sun.

Then with shocking suddenness, pop! The sun just seemed to jump up off the horizon. I tossed away my charred stump of a torch, closed my eyes, and spread my arms wide to welcome good old Mommy Sun.

It illuminated a scene out of some museum diorama. The plain stretched out before us, punctuated now with clumps of trees and sudden jutting rocks. The stream still wandered beside us. The woods were off to one side. The volcano was still smoking away, looking intimidating as it towered up above the plain.

And scattered about on that African-looking

savanna, where you might expect to see gazelles or wildebeest or lions, there was a small herd of Triceratops. They moved along calmly, maybe a hundred of them. Like an old-west buffalo herd, I guess. Only Buffalo Bill would have hung up his hat rather than go after these bad boys.

<Does the rising sun make humans feel more optimistic?> Ax asked.

"Yeah. Unless it's a school day," I said.

<We are the same. It doesn't make complete sense, but it does make me feel better. I can see. Seeing is useful.>

"Plus it blanks out that comet, and that thing was starting to bug me. On the other hand, I'm looking at a bunch of dinosaurs the size of cement trucks, so —"

<The comet bothered you? But not the flash of light?>

"Lightning. So what?"

<No, no. Not lightning. I assumed you knew. It was artificial in origin, not natural.>

It took me about five more steps before I said, "What?" I stopped. Jake stopped. Cassie stopped.

"Artificial?" Jake asked. "What do you mean, artificial? Doesn't that mean man-made? Or at least, *made*?"

<Yes, of course. The flash was not a naturally occurring phenomenon. It was all wrong for light-

ning. My stalk eyes are capable of seeing a little further into the ultraviolet and infrared spectra of light and —>

"Just tell us what it was!" Cassie yelled impatiently. That shocked us all. Cassie never yells. But then again, maybe she's just not a morning person.

<I believe it was an explosion. I would have thought it was a Dracon beam striking a target, only it was too blue.>

Jake took a deep breath. "Ax? Do me a favor. Don't assume we know these things, okay?"

<Yes, Prince Jake,> he said.

Jake looked at me. "You think Yeerks got transported back to this time with us somehow?"

<Prince Jake, I don't —>

"Don't call me prince," Jake said automatically.

"There weren't any Yeerks anywhere near that submarine when it blew up," I said. "Especially not any Yeerk spacecraft. I mean, come on, I think we'd have noticed."

<It isn't the Yeerks,> Ax said. <I assumed there must be some sort of highly advanced species of these dinosaurs. But it isn't the Yeerks.>

"Highly advanced dinosaurs?" I said. "Professor T-rex? I don't think so."

"Last night I saw some weird flashes far off," Jake said.

"Me, too," Cassie said. "I assumed they were lightning or something."

We resumed walking. "Ax-man, I think maybe you're just nuts."

<Me? Wrong? It is possible,> Ax said dubiously. <But the nature of the light certainly seemed to . . .>

He droned on for a while about the wavelengths and the retinal impact patterns and distance-sense and a lot of other Andalite stuff that humans would probably learn about someday.

I tuned it out. I was watching the Triceratops herd, which was off to our side now. I mean, come on, every little kid has a toy plastic Triceratops at some time. And here they were. Real. Actual dinosaurs moving along, munching the grass, occasionally using their huge long horns to dig up a tasty herb. It was cool. Set aside the fact that we had taken a big elevator ride about ten floors down on the food chain. It was still cool.

"Oh, man, look. I think we're coming up on some kind of big gorge or whatever," Jake said.

The prairie before us did seem to stop suddenly. The grass wasn't waving beyond a certain point.

"We'll have to go around," Cassie said.

"Why?" I wondered. "Where exactly is it we think we're going?"

"What do you want us to do?" Jake asked peevishly. "Sit down right here and start building a new civilization?"

"I'm just saying it's not like we have an appointment to be somewhere."

We marched on, unable to see the extent of the rift till we got close.

And then suddenly we could see. It was incredible. Like walking up on the Grand Canyon the first time. We were at the edge of a valley hundreds of feet deep and miles across. It gave me vertigo just standing there, like I might fall in.

And it would be a very long fall, with plenty of time to scream on the way down.

But that wasn't what really knocked the wind out of us. Because see, the valley wasn't empty. Down there, spread across a mile of valley floor, were glittering, shining buildings.

Buildings.

And hovering protectively above those buildings was something that looked an awful lot like a flying saucer.

CHAPTER 4

Tobias

"How's the wing?" Rachel asked.

<It itches. How are your feet?>

"They hurt all over again."

<Am I hurting your shoulder?>

"Nope. Not like you hurt my stomach when you opened me up like you were gutting a fish."

<I said I'm sorry. I've said it over and over.>

"I know. I'm cranky. I didn't exactly have a good night's sleep. I seem to remember having to morph the grizzly bear, only to have you come along and slice me up like I was a pepperoni pizza. Slice me up like I was a hunk of cheese."

I sighed. I tried to balance on Rachel's shoulder without digging my talons in. We'd ripped a patch of the dead Deinonychus's skin to cover her shoulder, but it wasn't staying on.

"Sliced me up like I was a ham," Rachel muttered. "Like I was bacon. And eggs. And some hash browns. Denny's. I'd give up shopping for a Denny's Grand Slam breakfast right now. The one with the pancakes. Get the hash browns as a side order. Two sausage links, two slices of bacon, two eggs over medium, you know? Not too soft and runny. I don't like them soft and runny. Maple syrup on the pancakes. Has to be maple. What kind of person puts boysenberry syrup on pancakes?"

<So I'm guessing you're hungry?>

She turned her icy blue eyes toward me. "Like a loaf of bread. That's how you sliced me up. Like a loaf of bread you get fresh from the bakery, all crusty and crispy and golden on the outside and soft and white and still-warm inside. And raspberry preserves. Has to be raspberry. I like Smuckers. A big jar of raspberry preserves with the seeds. I mean, what kind of baby has to have seedless preserves?"

I looked at her with my hawk's eyes. I was inches away. It was like looking at her through a microscope, practically. She hadn't slept, hadn't brushed her hair, and she was in a bad mood. But she looked great.

I looked away. What was the point? Jeez, my

own tiredness and hunger must be affecting me. I was starving. I could see little shrewlike mammals flitting between tree roots and cowering beneath ferns, but with a busted wing there was nothing I could do.

All I could do was watch the trees as we walked. We had left the Deinonychus pack behind in the night. As leader of the pack, I'd snarled at them till they backed away. I left them looking lost and stupid. But pretty soon they'd get around to choosing a new leader.

Rachel had acquired one of them. It hadn't been easy, but I'd been able to control the murderous creature long enough for her to touch him.

Now we were wandering along in the forest. Looking for food. Looking for Jake and the others. Looking for a clue of what to do.

We were entering an area with more vegetation now. There were clusters of palm trees here and there. Clumps of five or ten trees with some bushes around the base. It made me nervous. They blocked my view.

On the other hand . . . . <Hey, don't dates grow on trees?>

"Not according to my mom. She's thinking about dating again. You know, it's been awhile since the divorce and . . . oh. You mean like dates you eat? I guess they grow on trees."

<On date palms, right?>

"Like I know? Like I go food shopping out in the wild? Picking dates off trees and tomatoes off vines and corn out of, I don't know, corn trees?"

<Corn trees? Corn trees?>

"Oh, fine. I'm starving and you're picking on me because I'm not a farm girl like Cassie."

<We could go look at those palm trees. Maybe they have dates or coconuts in them. Something for you to eat, anyway.>

"I could use a rest. And some shade."

We headed toward the second nearest clump of trees. Two monstrously big Triceratops were over in the shade of the nearest trees. Supposedly they were peaceful plant-eaters. But they were big as elephants, with three-foot-long horns. So no matter how peaceful they were, I didn't want to share the shade with them.

<There's definitely something up in those trees,> I said. I could see pods of some sort clustered under the fanlike fronds.

We reached the shade of the tree. Rachel set me down on the ground and threw rocks till she knocked a pod down. It was brown, about the size of a coconut. She used another rock to bash it open. Inside was a whitish pulp.

"Well? What do you think?"

<I don't know. Most likely it won't kill you.>

Rachel made a face. She held a piece of the

pulp up to her nose. "Smells okay." Then she shrugged, popped some in her mouth and swallowed. "Hmm. Not bad."

<What's it taste like?> I asked. I gazed up jealously at the fruit. I was low down on the ground, not able to see much but the towering trees. But something caught my eye. Through the smooth trunks and riotous bushes, I saw something curved. It looked ridiculously like a handheld fan. Only much bigger. There were spines or spokes with brightly-patterned green and red fabric between them.

No, not fabric. Skin. But it had to be from something dead. It wasn't moving. Totally still.

<Rachel. I think there's something just on the other side of this clump of trees. See that — yaahhh!>

The fan had moved.

Rachel froze. "Please don't tell me it's another of your dinosaurs."

<When did they start being *my* dinosaurs? Let's just back away slowly.>

Rachel reached down to lift me up. "What is it?"

<I can't see enough of it to tell.>

We backed away, keeping our eyes firmly fixed on the spotted fan or sail. But as we backed away I realized Rachel's shoulder was getting tougher to hold on to.

<What are you doing?>

"I'm morphing," she said. "I'm hungry, you're hungry. Maybe we can take this guy down and have a nice big dinosaur breakfast."

<What? What?>

"I'm morphing that dannynockorus."

<Deinonychus?>

She couldn't answer. Her tongue was no longer human. Her skin was pebbly and rough. Her shoulder sloped downward and I jumped off to land in the grass.

I wasn't exactly happy with Rachel at that point. But at the same time, I wondered if maybe she was right. We had the Deinonychus morph. Why not use it?

I began to morph myself. Great, it would mean resetting my splint yet again. This was no way to heal. Then again, starving wasn't all that good for your health, either.

The breeze shifted. The skin and bone sail moved. It moved to catch the breeze. Why? I should know. There was some fact hiding just in the back of my head. What was I forgetting?

I pictured my toy dinosaurs. Tyrannosaurus rex, Brachiosaurus, Stegosaurus, Allosaurus, Spinosaurus.

Spinosaurus?

Big sail on its back. What about it? What was it like? What did it do? Was it an herbivore?

24

Moving!

CRASH! CRASH! Crrrrr-UNCH!

Up rose the sail as the Spinosaurus stood up. Crash went the bushes as it swiveled to look at us. Crunch went a tree trunk as it thrust its head through the trees to get a closer look at us. The head was bigger than Rachel.

She was just completing her Deinonychus morph. Would she be able to control the dinosaur's active instincts? She was more experienced at morphing than I was.

The Spinosaurus glared at us. Or at Rachel, at least.

<He's scared of us,> she said. <He's big, but he's probably just some great big prehistoric cow, right?>

<Rachel. Look at the teeth. Do those look like herbivore teeth?>

<Oh.>

The Spinosaurus rose up to its full standing height, looming up huge behind the trees. The curved sail on its back was more than five feet high. Tail to nose it was fifty feet long. It stood on two legs — smaller and weaker legs than a Tyrannosaurus, but plenty to move with.

The Spinosaurus was silent. It just stared as two Deinonychus emerged from a girl and a bird.

<We can still take him.>

That would be Rachel, of course. I'd never say

anything so stupid. <What are you, *crazy*? He weighs *tons*. We weigh *pounds*.>

<There's two of us. One of him.>

<One is plenty!>

<Okay. Then let's run away.>

<Now you're talking.>

We turned. We ran.

We ran right into the Spinosaurus's mate.

CHAPTER 5

Rachel

What could I do? I had to attack. The Deinonychus body was surging with power and deadly energy.

Then again, the Spinosaurus was way, way too big. To give you some idea, if we'd both been dogs, the Spinosaurus would be a German shepherd and I'd be a Chihuahua.

No choice. No way around the second Spinosaurus.

<Attack!> I yelled.

I leaped. The steel spring legs lifted me off the ground and I flew through the air, deadly raking claws outward. I was aiming for the Spinosaurus's exposed belly.

SLASH! With my oversized talons. Two bright red lines in the Spinosaurus's belly!

Two little lines that looked like something the Spinosaurus might put a Band-Aid on. The Spinosaurus looked puzzled. And then it looked annoyed. It ruffled its weird sail back and opened its jaws and looked at me like I had "Oscar Mayer" printed on my back.

<Okay, forget attack. We go back to plan "B." *Run*!>

And that's when I noticed the other creature step smoothly out from the bushes.

It walked on two legs. It was rough-textured, like it had really chapped skin. It was reddish in color. It had two big eyes and a small mouth, all of the same reddish-rust hue. It stood about eight feet tall. It was carrying a weapon.

It was not a dinosaur.

The creature raised the weapon and pointed it at the wounded and angry Spinosaurus. I saw no flash. Heard no explosion. But the Spinosaurus fell over. Like a redwood falling in the forest, it fell over.

WHAMMM!

The second Spinosaurus processed this and decided to go back to sleep.

Tobias and I stared at the rough-textured creature with the gun. <What the . . . what is *that*?>

<I don't know,> Tobias said. <But I can guarantee none of my toy dinosaurs ever carried guns.>

The creature gazed curiously at us with what seemed to be eyes, although they were mere indentations in its face. From its head a pair of antennae, flexible as whips, grew and began waving toward us.

Satisfied after a few seconds of this, the antennae were retracted.

"You may not kill those creatures. There are very few left. They are ours. All creatures are ours. All things are ours. What are *you*?" it asked in a rough, raspy, buzzing voice.

It was speaking English. Now, on *Star Trek* you see aliens speak English all the time. Like that would be normal. But in real life when you encounter an alien speaking English, it's just weird. You figure at the very least they should be speaking Russian or Japanese or something.

"Answer."

<We're . . . dinosaurs,> I said, feeling fairly idiotic.

"You speak now without making sound. Explain."

<Why don't *you* explain?> I said. <Who are you? What are you doing here? And how do you speak our language?>

"We hear while you are talking. Listening long time. Since night."

<How did this guy manage to follow us and listen in?> I asked Tobias.

<I don't know. I would have seen him.>

"Change to your other form."

<He's seen us morph.>

<What *are* you?> Tobias demanded.

"We are the Nesk. This is our planet. Change to your other form."

<Pushy, isn't he?> I said.

<He's got the gun.>

<I don't like him. He smells, for one thing. And the smell . . . something familiar about it. Something wrong. I can't quite remember. Can't quite place it. But something's wrong.>

"This weapon can cause creatures to become unconscious. This happened to the great beast you were attacking. But it can also cause death. Change into your other forms. Or I will cause your death."

The Nesk raised the weapon and pointed it at us.

Now, maybe I have to back down before a fifty-foot-long Spinosaurus. But I've faced plenty of pushy aliens with ray guns.

I knew this Nesk character with the ego problem would expect me to charge him, like a dinosaur. But I'm a human. Better yet, I'm a gymnast. So, just like on the balance beam, I spun on one leg and whipped my rigid tail into the Nesk.

<Take that!>

My tail hit hard. It slammed into the Nesk at his chest level. My tail broke him in two. The top half simply fell off. Like I'd chopped through a tree.

<Oh, my God!> I cried, horrified. I'd only intended to knock him down.

But then my horror changed tone. The severed lower body seemed to be dissolving. Breaking into thousands and tens of thousands of tiny squirming pieces!

And the fallen upper body was still holding the weapon. Raising it toward me again!

No time for pity. I lunged, mouth wide-open. I bit down on that raised hand.

It dissolved. Crumbled. I felt a squirming in my mouth. Then stinging, burning. I spit out the gun. It hit the dirt. And a wave made up of the Nesk's body parts raced to reach it.

My mouth was still alive with stinging and burning. The tiny reddish body parts began to crawl out of my jaw, up onto my muzzle. Up where my eyes could see them clearly.

Then I remembered that smell. The acrid

smell of a tunnel, the stink of deadly automatons racing to tear me apart.

Ants!

The Nesk was made up of millions and millions of ants.

CHAPTER 6
Cassie

"Okay, those buildings were *not* built by dinosaurs," Marco said.

Jake looked at Ax. "Ax? Do you have any idea what is going on here?"

Ax looked as puzzled as he was capable of looking. <You are sure this is not some unknown chapter of human history?>

"Ax, at this point humans aren't even a gleam in some tiny mammal's eye. We're a long, long way from seeing the first primate. Let alone an actual human. Could they be Andalites?"

<They are not Andalites,> Ax said. <We, too, have not yet evolved by this point. In fact, I believe our planet is still wandering between two

33

different stars, one of which will later go nova, but in such a way that the shock wave will —>

"A simple 'no' would do," Marco interrupted.

<They are certainly not Taxxons, Hork-Bajir, or even Yeerks. None of those species exists yet.>

"The Pemalites?" I suggested. We knew of the Pemalites from Erek. Erek looked and acted like a normal kid, but he was actually an android — a Chee — built by the extinct race called Pemalites.

Marco shook his head. "Erek told us when they arrived on Earth, the last Pemalites were dying. The Chee joined their essence or whatever with wolves. There aren't any wolves. We're probably tens of millions of years away from wolves, too."

"So who is hanging around on Earth in this era who can build cities and flying saucers?" Jake asked impatiently.

"Why don't I go ask them?" I said, pointing to the small city in the valley. "Or at least go check them out. My osprey morph would be perfect. There are birds in this era, so I shouldn't be too obvious."

Jake nodded. "Okay. That's what we'll do. We'll all go. But this just gets weirder and weirder."

"You know, only one of us has to go," I suggested. "Why don't I do it? You guys can all stay here for now."

Jake cocked an eyebrow. "What are you talking about?"

"Well, shouldn't we take the absolute minimum risk?"

Jake shook his head and kept looking at me like he couldn't figure me out.

"Look, we've already lost Rachel and Tobias," I blurted. "I lost my best friend. I don't want to lose . . . you know. Anyone else."

Marco looked like he was right on the verge of making a wisecrack. But he stopped. Still, I guess he just couldn't totally restrain himself, so he said, "Why don't I go with Cassie? Somehow I don't think it's *me* she's worried about losing." He gave Jake a sidelong smirk.

Jake rolled his eyes. "We are not going to lose anyone, okay? It's probably safer for us all to be in the air together. Here on the ground we have Big Rex to worry about."

It made sense. But it didn't make me feel any better. It had been just twenty-four hours since I'd last seen Rachel. I hadn't had all that much time to think about her. I'd been busy staying alive. And I guess the truth is, I almost didn't want to think about her really being gone.

But last night, in that terrible black chaos, blind, unable to tell where Jake's terrified cries were coming from, I just kept thinking, *No, it can't happen again. I can't lose Jake, too.*

Now here we were, staring down at what might be our only salvation in this dangerous world. But I was more worried than before. Maybe I trust animals more than civilization.

"Okay," I said. "But I get a bad feeling about this. See, this can't be right. There can't be a city down there. It doesn't make sense. There are no cities in the age of dinosaurs. And no flying saucers, either. I know we have to check it out, but we need to be careful."

I began to focus on my osprey morph. An osprey is a type of hawk that normally lives by water and eats fish.

Gray feather patterns began to appear on my skin. I saw my bare feet become talons, my arms twist into wing shapes. It was a morph I had done many times before. But it was a morph from a different world. This was a world where true birds seemed to be small in number.

There was a nice breeze blowing. And I could guess that there would be excellent thermals — warm updrafts — welling up from the steep valley walls.

<Everyone ready?> Jake asked.

<Look!> Marco yelled.

Half a dozen small dinosaurs, each standing

on two legs and no more than three feet high, goggled at us with huge yellow eyes.

<Let's fly,> Jake said.

The dinosaurs attacked at a run. A very fast run.

<I am getting so sick of this place,> Marco said as we flapped into the breeze and raced along on our talons.

I reached the edge of the cliff. I opened my wings and sprang out into the void. The tiny dinosaurs stopped at the edge and watched us go.

<This does seem to be a dangerous time in Earth's history,> Ax said. <It's a wonder humans ever evolved in such a dangerous world.>

<The dinosaurs were all gone before humans evolved,> I pointed out.

<All?> Ax asked, puzzled.

<Yeah. There were no dinosaurs by the time humans began to appear. They were all wiped out much earlier.>

<Unless you count the Flintstones,> Marco said. <"Flintstones, meet the Flintstones, they're the modern stone age family.">

I'd been right about the thermals. It felt good to be floating on a warm breeze. I know this seems crazy, but I somehow felt more at home in the osprey morph than my own human body. Humans just seemed so totally out of place in this era.

We flew toward the shining city in the valley. With osprey eyes I could see much more clearly. I saw buildings that rose in steep, smooth sweeps, like they'd grown from the bedrock. Windows were stuck in odd locations, some aiming out, others more like skylights. And there were fields planted with green and arranged in neat circles instead of rows.

<"From the town of Bedrock, they're a page right out of histo-ree,"> Marco sang.

As we got closer, I could see creatures of some sort. They looked a little like large — very large — crabs. Only with shells in a wild array of colors, deep blue, spring green, orange. And while on one side there was something very much like a large pincer, on the other side there was a pair of hands.

<Those are definitely not any species I know of,> Ax volunteered.

<They don't look friendly,> Marco said.

<Marco, how can you possibly —>

WHAM!

Something hit me! I was tumbling through the air. I fell ten feet, opened my wings again and veered into a breeze. I caught air. Nothing broken. <Jake!> I cried.

<Look out, it's coming around again!> Jake yelled.

I turned my head just in time to see it fill my

38

entire field of vision. Like some monstrous bat. Green-and-yellow leather wings twenty feet across. An impossibly long, bony head.

<I can't believe something that big could sneak up on me,> I said.

<There are more,> Ax said tersely.

They were dropping from caves in the valley wall. Three, four, six of them. They opened their wide leather wings and swooped toward us.

CHAPTER 7

Tobias

They swarmed toward Rachel. Millions of ants. And a group of them was already reforming around the weapon, forming a sort of hand to raise it high and aim it.

I had a very low-tech idea of how to deal with that. I leaped. I landed with both feet on the ants around the weapon. And I began to stomp.

I stomped like mad with my Deinonychus feet. They weren't great feet for stomping because they were basically built like bird feet. But they were fast. I was stomping at a rate of several stomps per second. And whatever kind of super-alien ants these might be, they couldn't stand some man-sized dinosaur stomping on them.

The Nesk broke and ran. I roared in triumph

and turned to Rachel. She was avidly licking the ants off her with her long tongue.

<What on or off the Earth was that?> I said.

<I don't even want to know,> Rachel said. <I'll tell you something about your Cretaceous Park here, though. I don't like it. It's grinding my last nerve. Not bad enough we have murderous dinosaurs everywhere. Noooo, we have to have ant-creatures from planet Zeptron!>

<Zeptron?>

<It's the first word that came to mind, all right? You want to grind my nerves, too?>

<Nope. Definitely not. But maybe we should —>

Ch-ch-ch-CHEEEEEW! Ch-ch-ch-CHEEEEEW! Ch-ch-ch-CHEEEEEW!

The ground beside me exploded, like it had been ripped by an invisible plow. I jumped. Another plow mark just behind me! I saw movement. And there, racing toward us across the plain, was a gleaming, silver craft. Maybe twice the size of a Bug fighter, but shaped like an elongated pyramid, long end forward.

Ch-ch-ch-CHEEEEEW! Ch-ch-ch-CHEEEEEW! Ch-ch-ch-CHEEEEEW!

The ship fired again and blew two more five-foot-long furrows in the ground.

<Run!> Rachel said.

<Run!> I agreed.

We ran. Deinonychus can run when it wants to. Very fast. Maybe twenty miles an hour. Too bad the silver pyramid was about a thousand times faster.

But it hesitated. I glanced back and saw it pause over the spot where we'd been. A sort of tube with a scoop on the end lowered to the ground. And I swear it vacuumed up the ants we'd scattered.

It came after us again. We dodged and the craft fired, ripping tear after tear in the ground around us.

<They're playing with us!> I yelled.

<I don't like the game,> Rachel said.

<No, I mean, like cat and mouse. They can hit us any time. They're missing on purpose. They're enjoying this.>

<Or else they're herding us,> Rachel said grimly. <They want us to keep going this way.>

Directly ahead of us was a small herd of Triceratops. Of course, small only referred to the number of animals in the herd. Each one was the size of an elephant.

<I have to be able to see what's up ahead, up past that herd,> I said. <I'm gonna leapfrog!>

<What?>

I didn't have time to explain. We reached the Triceratops. One huge bull swung his three-foot-long horns toward us in challenge. I sidestepped him and leaped onto the back of an equally big but less alert female.

I leaped! Soared through the air, coiled my legs, timed it just right to slam my legs down on the Triceratops's back, bounced off her, and hurtled another ten feet in the air.

From up there I could see the trap. Then I was falling.

WHUMPF!

I hit, rolled, jumped up and yelled, <You were right, it's a trap! There's a whole wall of them. A whole wall of ants! Billions! The only way out is left, but there's a sheer drop there. Can't tell how deep.>

<Great! A sheer drop or a wall of space ants! Nice choice.>

<On the count of three, we dodge left and keep going no matter what. One . . . two . . .>

<Three!> Rachel yelled.

We hauled left.

Ch-ch-ch-CHEEWWW!

Explosions of earth and rock cut across our path but I didn't care. I'd seen what was up ahead. This was better.

We raced, panting and gasping, toward what looked to us like the end of the world. A sudden gap. An emptiness.

<What is it the sky divers always say before they jump?> I asked.

<Geronimo!> Rachel yelled.

<Yeah, that's it,> I said and leaped into emptiness. Rachel was three seconds behind me.

It might have been a five foot drop. It might have been ten feet. Unfortunately, it was about five hundred feet.

<Aaaaaaaahhhhhhh!> I cried.

<Aaaaaaaahhhhhhh!> Rachel agreed.

Falling, falling, spinning out of control, no time to morph. I was going to die. I would be slammed against the ground far below and die.

But even as I spun crying through the air, I swear I saw bright buildings. And then, much closer, a bird. A very familiar bird. Back in my own world I have to watch out for peregrine falcons. See, every now and then one of them will actually take a shot at a hawk.

It was like some insane joke. Like fate was trying to get a good laugh at me. Dinosaurs, aliens, and now my old nemesis, a peregrine falcon.

Then I saw the other set of wings.

The twenty-five-foot-wide wings and bony chisel-head of a creature no human had ever seen before.

Pteranodon! I thought. *I used to play with you.*

CHAPTER 8
Jake

The flying dinosaurs were above us. That was the problem. We were more maneuverable, but they had the altitude. And slowly but surely, by circling above us, they were forcing us down and down. Down toward the glimmering city below us.

I looked in every direction. How to get away? How to get out from under this trap?

The silver flying saucer was now only twenty feet below us, the highest spires of the alien city just another thirty feet lower than that.

We were trapped. If we went up, the flying dinosaurs. If we went down, the city full of bright, bizarre, two-handed crabs.

<Back to the cliff wall,> I said. <The ther-

mals will be strongest there. Maybe we can get enough lift to outrun them straight up!>

We curved back toward the cliff wall. Four of us. Cassie and Marco in osprey morph, Ax as a northern harrier, and me, a peregrine falcon.

We flapped at full speed for the cliffs. I could see colonies of the flying dinosaurs nesting there on crags in shallow caves. More were taking wing.

Stupid! I was leading everyone right back toward more of the creatures. And yet it might just work.

<Get ready everyone! Hug that cliff wall!>

I was ten seconds from slamming right into the cliff. Five. Three!

Something falling toward me! Quick turn left. Two dinosaurs, looking like miniature tyrannosaurs, were falling, kicking and scrabbling. They'd leaped off the cliff! A shower of falling rock was dislodged behind them.

They fell. The leather-winged flying dinosaurs closed in on us. In a flash of swift movement, one of the falling dinosaurs reached out with its little forepaw and snagged one of the leather wings! To my utter amazement, I saw him reach with his free claw to grab the other wing tip.

The dinosaur spread the wings as far as it could. Twenty feet of leathery wing. Like a hang glider. Just enough to glide with.

The second dinosaur caught a leg on a jutting rock. It slowed the fall, but only for a second, then it tumbled away. But now there was enough time. The dinosaur with the living hang glider swept toward it.

<Rachel, get ready to grab something!> the first dinosaur yelled.

It was as if someone had stuck a thousand volt wire in my ear.

<Tobias?>

<Jake?>

WHAM! Tobias aimed for Rachel and slammed into her. Rachel was knocked into the cliff wall. Tobias was able to catch a ledge. Rachel scrabbled frantically, but kept missing her hold. She tumbled into a nest of the flying dinosaurs.

There was a furious falling, rattling, screaming, dirt-flying tussle that rolled down the cliff, but when the dust cleared, there was Rachel . . . or at least a dinosaur . . . holding tight to the legs of one big leather wing and the neck of another.

She dragged them down the side of that cliff, both of them flapping madly.

I dove after her, calling to the others.

Down, down, down. Then WHAM!

She landed. But not on the valley floor. She landed in midair. She was crumpled on what looked like midair. And the two tattered, leather wings were beside her. Also in midair.

<Force field!> Ax yelled.

I pulled up, just as my breastbone scraped along what seemed like a pure, clear glass roof.

The others swooped down and landed on the force field.

<Rachel?> Cassie cried. <Is that you?!>

<Of course, it's me,> Rachel said, sounding as if the idea of her being some little dinosaur who'd just jumped off a cliff, grabbed a pair of giant leather-wing dinosaurs and landed on an alien force field was totally normal. <Who else would it be?>

We were all treated to the utterly bizarre sight of an osprey attempting to hug a dinosaur.

<I know this is kind of obvious,> Marco began, <but you're both alive!>

<Of course,> Tobias said. <You think getting eaten by a Kronosaurus was going to kill us? Nah. Or being chased by a pack of Deinonychus?>

<What are you, Dinosaur-boy?> Marco asked.

<Now you know what I've been putting up with since yesterday,> Rachel said. <This-a-saurus and that-a-saurus. Tobias rattles them off like they were, I don't know, like any normal person would rattle off the names of major clothing designers.>

48

<What do you call the morphs you're in?> I asked.

<Deinonychus. And those flying reptiles there are Pteranodons,> Tobias said. <Am I the only person who ever played with dinosaurs when I was little?>

<Hey. There are buildings down there,> Rachel said. <What's going on? We were being chased by these aliens who are ants but who can join together to form bodies and carry guns. He . . . or they . . . said they were the Nesk.>

Every eye turned to Ax. He sounded a little exasperated. <I don't know. Never heard of them. We are millions of years in the past, you know. I cannot be expected to know every species in the history of the galaxy.>

<At least sixty-five million years in the past,> Tobias said. <Cretaceous Age. The last age of dinosaurs.>

Marco moaned. <Oh, man. Sixty-five million years! I thought it was just maybe six or seven million years. I was holding out hope that we'd find some primitive people. You know, like in that old movie *Quest for Fire*? Only the babe tribe, not the hairy tribe. There would be this primitive tribe and because of my superior knowledge I would become their ruler.>

<Your superior knowledge of *what*, Marco? Your superior knowledge of Spider-Man's super

powers?> Rachel asked scornfully. <You run into a tribe of Neanderthals, you'd end up being their pet monkey.>

Everyone laughed. Even Marco. It was good having the group together again. But I had to get us moving.

<Excuse me, but we seem to be standing on a force field a hundred feet or so above a valley filled with aliens. Maybe we should leave. Unfortunately, there are still a bunch of mad Pteranodons above us.>

<And maybe a small ship full of those Nesk whatevers,> Tobias pointed out. <Are they the same aliens who are down in this valley?>

<No,> a voice said. <The Nesk and the Mercora are not the same.>

I looked at Ax. He looked at me. Everyone looked at everyone else. None of us had spoken. None of us even knew the word "mercora."

Out across the force field, they appeared very gradually. At first there was just a ripple in the air, then a sort of bad TV picture full of static. Then the picture was clear and real and three-dimensional.

<A localized, force-field-derived sensor shield!> Ax said enthusiastically. <Excellent!>

We were face-to-face with the aliens. Not that we could be sure where the face was, exactly.

CHAPTER 9

Ax

We Andalites know more about alien races than anyone in the galaxy. We have been in space longer and traveled farther. Plus, we are scientists as well as warriors, so when we find a new race we study it. As opposed to wiping it out or enslaving it, as the Yeerks do.

We know of the Gedds and Hork-Bajir and Taxxons, the Korla, the Skrit Na, the humans, and many, many others.

But this race, these Mercora, were just strange. For one thing, they were not at all symmetrical.

There were three of the creatures. They moved upon seven legs. Four on one side, three on the other. To make matters worse, the four legs were larger than the three. So they scuttled sideways in the direction of the small legs.

They stood about half the height of a tall human, and seven or eight feet wide.

On the side with the four big legs, there was a sort of three-way pincer claw. It looked very powerful. It looked like the sort of thing I would not want to have to fight against.

On the other side, the weak side, there were two arms similar to my own, but even stronger than human arms. The arms ended in long, tapered, delicate fingers.

There were a lot of eyes. They kept opening and shutting, one or two or three at a time. They were each hidden beneath tiny trap doors in the Mercora's exoskeleton or shell. Eyes were forever appearing and disappearing. It was very, very distracting.

<Finally,> Marco muttered. <Someone who can win a staring contest with Ax.>

<We are the Mercora,> one of them said in thought-speak. <We are immigrants to this planet. We thought we had encountered most of the many species on this planet. But we have never encountered an intelligent species here before.>

<They think we're intelligent,> Rachel whispered. <So, Marco, keep quiet. We don't want them to learn the truth.>

It is strange the way humans will resort to what they call humor when they are frightened. Once again it struck me as strange that they had risen to dominate the very dangerous and hostile environment of Earth. I wondered how well they would have fared if they had coexisted with the dinosaurs.

<May I ask what you call yourselves?> the Mercora spokesman said.

<Is it safe to tell them the truth?> Cassie asked us all privately.

<We're sixty-five million years before the first Yeerk will show up on Earth,> Prince Jake said. <And maybe these Mercora can help us get back home.>

Prince Jake stepped forward. As well as a falcon walking on a force field could step. <We are called humans. Except for this one . . .> He tilted his head toward me. <He is an Andalite.>

The Mercora looked confused. Maybe. It was hard to tell. I can barely interpret human facial expressions. But in any case it opened and closed groups of eyes in rapid succession.

<Do you inhabit this continent?>

<Well . . .> Prince Jake said. <That's kind of a long story. Um, Ax? You probably can explain better than I can.>

<Yes, Prince Jake. We are from the future,> I said.

<Hey, that's a *much* better explanation than Jake could have come up with,> Marco said. <"We are from the future." Thank goodness we have a brilliant alien Space-boy here who can explain things.>

<The future?> the Mercora said. <How far in the future?>

<A . . . a long, long way,> I responded.

<Not to get all technical or anything,> Marco said dryly. <Look, sir, ma'am, whatever you are, Mr. or Ms. Mercora, we aren't what we seem. If you promise not to tell some people who won't even exist for another sixty-five million years, we'll show you, okay?>

<Yeah, let's do it,> Prince Jake said. <What do we have to lose?>

<Aside from our lives,> Rachel added dryly.

<My decision,> Prince Jake said heavily. <I think we should demorph.>

I began to do so. It must have been a bizarre sight for the Mercora. They each opened a startling number of eyes. Tobias went from dinosaur to hawk. Rachel from dinosaur to human. Cassie, Marco, and Prince Jake from bird to human. And I morphed from bird to Andalite.

<As you see,> I explained, <we are two different species. They are human. I am Andalite.>

<And what is he?> the Mercora asked, pointing both hands at Tobias.

<He is a human, but he suffered an accident and was trapped in his morph.>

<You are a strange species,> the Mercora said. <But you are welcome as long as you come in peace and do not serve the Nesk.>

"It was the Nesk that chased us here," Rachel said.

<Now it speaks with sound!> the Mercora commented.

"Yes, *it* does that when it's not in morph," Rachel said. "I get the idea you and the Nesk don't get along."

<They are attempting to destroy us. They want this planet for themselves. We do not wish to leave. This is our world now. Our original planet was destroyed when our sun was drawn toward a black hole. We are all that is left of the Mercora. And we cannot leave this planet. Not that we would ever wish to. It is wonderful. Wonderful. And it will be our home forever.>

A second Mercora spoke up. <What planet in the future are you from, you humans and Andalites?>

Cassie started to answer. "Actually, we're from Earth. Which is our name for —"

Suddenly she fell silent and looked shocked. Tobias was staring intensely at her. And then he spoke to me in the personal, private thought-speak whisper he'd used to silence Cassie. A whisper the Mercora could not hear.

<No one tell them we're from this planet,> Tobias said. <Hear me? No one tells them this is our planet.>

For a moment I was surprised. Slowly, understanding dawned on me.

The Mercora were wrong: They were not going to be a part of Earth's future. They were destined either to leave . . . or to be destroyed.

CHAPTER 10

Marco

"You know, for being big, lopsided crabs with way too many eyeballs, these guys are really all right," I said, as I reclined against a force field shaped into an easy chair and tinted an attractive blue.

A day had gone by. The Mercora had speed-healed Tobias's busted wing, fed us, custom-designed a place for us to stay, and even attempted to make clothing for us. I was feeling pretty relaxed, gazing out of a window down at the Mercora who were busily working in the fields tending their broccoli.

Yes, broccoli. Turns out broccoli isn't even from Earth originally. The Mercora imported it from their home planet. Which explains a lot, I think.

"We have a nice apartment. We have food. Sadly, it's all vegetables, but hey, later we can introduce the concept of the McRex: two all-Tyrannosaurus patties, special sauce, lettuce, cheese, pickles, onions on a sesame seed bun. The McRex, the Quarter Tonner with cheese. And not to be impolite about our new pals here, but I'll bet these Mercora would be pretty tasty served with some melted butter."

"What are we *doing* here?" Rachel demanded. "What are we going to do, just sit around on these La-Z-Boy force fields, eat broccoli, and listen to Marco babble like an idiot?"

That's when Ax came back in the room. He'd been talking to the Mercora. They found it easier communicating with him because he uses thought-speak like they do.

<I have questioned the Mercora,> Ax announced. <In order to repair the *Sario Rip* and snap us back to our own time, they say — and I agree — that we would need an explosion of great power. At least as great as the power of that fusion weapon aboard the submarine. The Mercora point out that such an explosion would annihilate this entire settlement.>

58

"So? We do the explosion out in the country-side," Rachel said.

"And wipe out a few hundred thousand di-nosaurs?" Cassie said.

"Besides," Jake pointed out, "the Mercora have already told us they don't control the coun-tryside. Out there, beyond the force field, the Nesk are more powerful."

I reached down and snagged a carrot stick from a little ice bowl. At least carrots were from Earth. I munched it, thought about making a Bugs Bunny joke, decided the joke I had in mind wasn't all that funny, then said, "Look, we all want to get back, right? Our families. My dad. But either we can or we can't. If we can't, ab-solutely *can't*, then maybe we should just try and make the best of this."

Ax came over to stand by the window. He looked out with his main eyes. One stalk eye was pointed at me. The other was pointed toward the rest of the group. <The Mercora don't use explo-sive weapons, anyway. They would not have any-thing powerful enough. However . . .>

I saw Rachel's head snap around. "However *what*?"

<However, they say the Nesk do have large explosive weapons. They say the Nesk have a base twenty miles away. It is very well defended.

No Mercora ship could hope to get close. They have a standoff. The Nesk cannot penetrate this valley through the force field. The Mercora cannot eliminate the Nesk base.>

"Are you making a suggestion?" Jake asked Ax.

<No. Just reporting what I have learned from talking with the Mercora.>

I sat up. I looked Ax in the eye — the eye pointed toward me, that is. "Okay, what are you *not* mentioning?"

Ax turned back to the group, but kept that one eyeball on me. <The Nesk are scavengers. The ships they fly, the weapons they use, are all modeled on the tools of races the Nesk have defeated. The Nesk have learned to mimic the bodies and shapes of these other races in order to fire the weapons and fly the ships. The Nesk believe the dinosaurs belong to them. As their property. They believe this planet belongs to them. But they cannot tolerate the existence of other sentient, intelligent species. They are determined to wipe out the Mercora.>

"You know, it doesn't matter if they're space ants or plain old Earth ants, ants are just not nice people," I said, and munched a second carrot.

Rachel rolled her eyes. "Ants are not nice people? There's a brilliant comment."

"Okay," Jake said. "So we have two alien

races fighting to control Earth. The Mercora seem basically harmless. They just want to plant broccoli —"

"That's not harmless," I muttered.

"— and live here in their valley. The Nesk, on the other hand, are aggressive and murderous. The Mercora can't help us. The Nesk maybe could help us, but won't because, after all, we're an intelligent species, too, and they don't like competition."

"Send Marco to talk to the Nesk," Rachel suggested brightly. "They won't mind him."

"Ha. Haha and also ha," I said. "Look, to get serious here, the Nesk didn't smoke that Spinosaurus that was gonna eat Rachel and Tobias, right?"

Tobias stopped preening his feathers. He was perched on the force-field table, having enjoyed a tasty prehistoric rat brought for him by the thoughtful Mercora.

<They knocked it out. It was alive, though.>

"Exactly. So I guess the Nesk don't mind dinosaurs. I mean, okay, if a Mercora flying saucer shows up at the Nesk home base, they blast it. But what if a whole different kind of army shows up there?"

Rachel suddenly grabbed my shoulder so enthusiastically it hurt. "It's a miracle! Marco actually came up with a good idea. We can morph dinosaurs and stomp on in there, set off some big honkin' explosion and maybe undo this *Sario Rip* of Ax's!"

<It is not my *Sario* —> Ax began.

"Wait a minute, why are we attacking the Nesk?" Cassie demanded. "Just because we don't like them doesn't mean we take up sides in the Mercora–Nesk war."

"Look," I said, prying Rachel's gymnast-strong fingers off my collarbone. "We need a big explosion to hopefully close the *Sario Rip.* The Nesk have things that go 'boom.' And they aren't expecting a bunch of dinosaurs to show up asking to borrow a cup of plutonium, right? Now, that's not too complicated."

<Plutonium?> Ax snorted like I'd made a joke. <Oh, you're serious. But maybe the Nesk have slightly more advanced explosives.>

"What are you talking about?" Cassie cried. "We can't just go around picking fights like this. We all want to get back home. But we're sixty-five million years in the past. And we are not supposed to be here. Anything we do could end up changing the course of history in some terrible way."

"Ah," Jake said, nodding.

"We could do something that ends up totally altering the future without even knowing it,"

Cassie said. "We could . . . I don't know, we could do *something*! Something wrong."

"We could change the future so that Hanson would never have existed," I said. "I say we try!"

"You going to try and wipe out *every* guy who's cuter than you, Marco?" Rachel asked. "That's half the human race."

"Look, we can't go messing with the future," Cassie said. "It's too complicated. Too many consequences."

<Too late,> Tobias said, speaking up for the first time. <We have Homo sapiens alive here in this timeline. Not to mention me. Whatever I am. See this rat I just ate? That could have been the rat that will pass on the genetic material that someday grows a smarter rat. And fifty million years from now, maybe that's the DNA, the stuff that's needed to push the earliest primate over the top. I may have wiped out the human race.> He looked down at the fur and bones. <And it wasn't even a very good rat. Too thin and stringy.>

One by one, we all looked at Jake.

"Oh, puh-leeze! I'm supposed to decide things that may wipe out the human race?"

"You're Batman," I said. "I'm just Robin. The boy wonder," I added with a leer at Rachel.

Jake shrugged. "What are we supposed to do?

Sit here and grow old, eating broccoli with the crab people? Never even try to go home?"

<There is one other consideration,> Ax said. <We are here. Which means we *were* here, sixty-five million years in Earth's past. In other words, maybe our presence here is vital to the future. Maybe we did something that *caused* the future to happen the way it happened.>

"Is anyone else's head exploding from all this?" I asked.

"Great," Jake said, stomping a few steps in frustration, then turning around again. "So if I suggest we attack the Nesk, maybe that wipes out the future. And if I suggest *not* to attack the Nesk, that could also wipe out the future. Excellent. Perfect. As long as it's all nice and clear."

<*This* decision may not be clear,> Tobias said quietly. <But another decision may be so obvious we can't ignore it.>

No one asked what he meant because at that point some Mercora showed up with more food. But I filed away his words. I filed them away in my head and I had the definite feeling I'd be double-clicking on that file again.

CHAPTER 11

Ax

I am often amazed at Prince Jake's ability to make decisions. I call him my prince because any Andalite warrior needs a prince to serve. But I know that he is just a human youth, as I am an Andalite youth.

And yet he is very impressive for a human youth. He understands instinctively that making no decision is also a decision. So he accepts the responsibility.

If he were an Andalite I have no doubt he would become a true prince. Still, he does very well for a human.

In the end, we decided to "go for it." That is a human expression. As I understand it, the expression means that without having any clear

65

idea of why we should do something, we would do it anyway.

We would attack at dawn. I asked why dawn.

"Tradition," Marco said. "You do shoot-outs at high noon, you stretch in the seventh inning, you attack at dawn."

Like much of human thinking, this is a mystery to me.

"You also get executed at dawn," Cassie said.

"Thank you, Cassie, for that bit of optimism."

We had explained our plan to the Mercora. They approved. We would attack the Nesk home base and seize an explosive weapon. A bomb. A "nuke," as my human friends said. Then we would return to the ocean and attempt to explode this "nuke" in such a way that it would close the *Sario Rip* and return us to our own time.

I hoped the Mercora would have some idea how to do this. I certainly didn't. We learned about *Sario Rips* in school. But I wasn't really paying attention that day, and I can't be expected to remember all the things I learned in school. Can I?

I was sure my human friends understood this. But to be absolutely sure, I mentioned it as we sped through the night toward the Nesk base aboard a ground-hugging Mercora transport.

<Prince Jake, you do understand that I have

no idea precisely how or where or when to set off an explosion that will seal the *Sario Rip*?>

"What? *What?!*"

I was mistaken. It was clear from the expression he made with his human mouth, and the way his voice became loud and rose at the end toward a sort of shriek, and also by the way his eyes alternately narrowed and expanded, that Prince Jake had not been entirely clear on this point.

<I know that we should probably create an explosion. I don't know exactly when or where. Although it should be near the point where we first emerged into this world. I am sure of that. Mostly.>

"Don't you think you might have mentioned this earlier?" Marco said. "Like *before* we signed on for this suicide mission?"

"Look, we need the nuke, right?" Rachel said. "One way or the other, we need the nuke. So let's do it."

"Oh, I hate when she says 'let's do it,'" Marco moaned. "I've changed my mind now. I can learn to like broccoli."

One of the three Mercora with us scuttled around to face us. It opened a half dozen eyes in a rapid flutter. <We are close to the place we will leave you. It is on the edge of the Nesk defensive grid. As close as we can go. Approximately point

67

zero zero zero zero two six eight light seconds from the base.>

"Which would be . . . ?" Prince Jake asked me.

<Approximately five of your miles,> I translated.

"Five miles? In the dark? Here in Cretaceous Park?" Marco said. "That's kind of a hike, isn't it?"

But the Mercora were firm. Any closer and the transport would be spotted and fired on. Success depended on surprise. We were to appear to be any bunch of wandering dinosaurs. Harmless to the Nesk.

The transport came to rest amid jumbled rocks. The Mercora were very advanced when it came to force fields. But their ships were clunky and slow, compared to Andalite technology. Or what would be Andalite technology in sixty-five million years.

It was very dark outside. The Mercora kept their exterior ship's lights low. And as I trotted down the ramp, the brightest thing around was the comet. It was shockingly close now. The tail would certainly brush the planet as it passed.

Dawn was still two hours away. We were to travel the five miles to the Nesk base in that time and be ready to move in as soon as the sun rose on the horizon.

<Take this, Andalite,> the Mercora copilot said. With one of his hands he gave me a small communicator.

<A thought-speak communicator?>

<Yes. The humans could not use it, but you will be able to.>

<What is its purpose?>

<You can inform us how the mission goes,> the Mercora said.

<Are you offering to help?>

<No. We cannot risk our limited ships and equipment.>

I nodded as if I understood. But I was puzzled. The Mercora scuttled back aboard their ship. It lifted silently off the ground with an intriguing violet glow, then sped away into the darkness.

I don't know about the humans, but I felt extremely lonely. I am always alone, being the only Andalite on planet Earth. But now I was more alone than that. My own people would not exist for tens of millions of years.

We were in the dark, a very deep darkness, beneath the glowing comet, in a past that was not my own, in a past filled with destructive monsters.

From far off I heard, "Hunh-huhnroooaaarrr."

Then Prince Jake said, "Okay, let's morph."

CHAPTER 12

Cassie

I didn't want to be here. I didn't want to be doing this. We didn't really have a plan. We didn't truly know what we were doing. But I couldn't sit it out. No way. Not when my friends were facing danger.

I looked up. The comet was shockingly big in the sky. The tail spread a quarter of the distance from horizon to horizon. It was beautiful. But it frightened me. Ahead, in the direction of the Nesk base, there was a slight, reddish glow that seemed to hover in the air. I realized it was the summit of the volcano.

"Okay, let's morph," Jake said.

There was no doubt which morph he meant.

This was not a place for my osprey or my dolphin, my skunk or even my wolf. This was dinosaur country. I had only one morph that was useful in this situation.

Tyrannosaurus rex. The tyrant lizard king.

In all of Earth's history, all the millions of years and all the billions of animals that have come and gone, this one single creature was the most powerful predator.

"I can't believe I'm stuck in a lousy little Deinonychus morph," Rachel complained. "You guys all get to do Big Daddy, and Tobias and I have to be Babysaurus."

"I wish I wasn't doing it," I said.

"Yeah, right," Rachel snorted.

There are some things about Rachel I still don't understand. And things about me that must mystify her, I guess. Rachel loves the big predator morphs. I don't. I never want to hurt anyone or anything. Not even when I have to. Not even when there's no choice.

"Tell you one thing," Marco said. "If you're gonna walk around in the dark here in Cretaceous world, you want to be carrying the big guns. And Big Rex is the biggest."

"I guess I'd rather have the Mercora's force fields," I said. "I like the way they do things: They protect themselves without having to be so violent."

<They don't seem to object to our being violent *for* them,> Tobias said.

I looked to see him in the dark. He was already morphing. A man-sized dinosaur was growing from a bird.

"Let's just do this, all right?" Marco said impatiently. "I've been on the wrong end of a fight with a Tyrannosaurus, okay? I don't want to be standing around here debating in the dark when another one shows up looking for an early breakfast."

Jake said, "Rachel, Tobias, you guys keep an eye on us. These are new morphs for the four of us. We may have some trouble adjusting."

I took a deep breath. I guess I'd been hoping somehow we'd change our minds. But the time had come.

I focused my mind on the Tyrannosaurus whose DNA was within me. And I let the changes begin.

I expected to sprout right up. But the first changes were more subtle. My skin became rough and slightly loose. Like it didn't quite fit. Lizard skin. Crocodile skin.

My hands split in two. My thumb and next two fingers melted together. My two smaller fingers did the same. And then the bones grew out through the lizard flesh. The finger bones grew and came to a point, two small but wicked claws.

I felt my bones grow thick and massive. My pelvis bone swelled out against my flesh. I thought it would break through. But then I realized the growing had started. I was rising up, up from the ground.

My legs were thickening, growing. Muscle layered over muscle. Muscles much bigger than my own human body. Bone and muscle, bone and muscle.

My spine began to stretch, with a squeaking sound that radiated through my head. The base of my spine stretched out and out, longer and longer, five feet, six, eight, ten feet! And longer still.

My feet grew, spreading wide into three massive toes, each ending in a ripping, rending claw. I felt my weight settle on those feet, felt my claws sink into the moist soil as I grew by tons with each passing moment.

But for all that, it was the Tyrannosaurus's head that shocked me the most. My jaw went from being measured in inches to being measured in feet. The bones grew dense and heavy. The muscles rippled beneath the gravel skin. My face bulged out and out and out. My eyes spread apart, blurring everything until they had reached their proper location, facing forward.

My head expanded, grew in every direction. Bigger, always bigger! I was towering above the ground now. Huge! I balanced on my powerful legs, tail out behind me, body forward, poised.

And then, at last, came my teeth. I felt the itching in my mouth as my pathetically tiny, my ridiculous human, teeth grew. From a quarter inch to an inch, to three inches, to six, seven!

New teeth appeared. Twice my normal number. They sprouted from the bones of my massive jaws.

And I was complete. More than forty feet from head to tail: the length of a bus. Eighteen feet tall: the height of a two-story house. Seven tons of bone and muscle: the weight of five cars.

Power and speed and destruction made flesh. Power the world had never seen before and would never see again.

I had become Tyrannosaurus rex.

King of the dinosaurs.

CHAPTER 13

Marco

Surrounded! I was surrounded by enemies! I could see them looming up around me. They would fight me for food. They would steal prey. They had entered my territory!

"RRRRROOOAAARRR!" I bellowed in rage.

"HeeeRRRROOOOAAAARRR!" they answered, one by one.

Four of us together in one place. Impossible! My territory. Mine!

"HeeeRRRROOOOAAAARRR!" I raged.

But the others did not run away. They roared back at me. Four huge voices cried, "Outrage!" We bellowed and roared our threats, but no one ran away.

75

I stamped my feet, one after the other. I swung my tail back and forth.

The others did the same. They stamped their feet at me. At each other. Tails were swishing madly, ripping bushes and small trees out of the ground. The threat display was clear. Someone should back down. The only alternative was to do battle.

"HeeeRRRROOOOAAAARRR!" we each cried, swaying as we stomped, swishing our tails, tossing our heads, opening our mouths wide to display our deadly teeth.

Then . . . a scent.

We each caught it at the same time. The bellowing stopped. I turned my head toward the smell. Darkness. But the scent was there: living flesh. Prey.

<You guys, you're losing it! Jake, Cassie, Marco, you guys are losing it!>

There was prey just a few feet away. Two smaller creatures. Only two of them, and four of us. Not enough prey. The others would try to take them.

I leaped!

The little dinosaurs turned and ran. I was after them!

<Jake! Ax! Marco, you idiot! You guys are caught up in the morph! That's us you're chasing.>

Noises in my head. Meaningless. Running

now, the chase was on! But the others like me were still there. Running, too. Trying to steal my prey!

<You guys are grinding my nerves! You're hunting us.>

<Rachel, we can't outrun them! But we can out-turn them, I bet.>

<Oh, this is so not fun! I'm gonna end up being breakfast for Marco. Talk about humiliation. When I say "now!" we double back on them!>

<Yeah.>

More sounds in my head. Strange. Disturbing.

<Now!>

The two swift, small creatures suddenly stopped and ran straight for me. In a flash, they were past. I stopped. I blinked. I was confused.

But then I smelled new prey. More this time! Close by. The wind was in my face. I knew this was a good thing. When the wind was in my face, the prey did not flee as quickly.

I quickly forgot the two small creatures and advanced toward the herd I smelled up ahead in the darkness.

<I have never seen a morph take over this totally.>

<I know. I'm starting to worry.>

<Jake! It's me, Rachel. Snap out of it. Cassie, buddy. It's me, Rachel. You're being controlled by the morph.>

The prey was close now. Yes, I could smell them. I glanced at the others like myself. Marching beside me through the darkness. Many prey this time. Enough for all.

Closer . . . closer . . .

Attack!

I bounded forward at full speed. Attack! Tail out behind me, head held forward, I raced toward the helpless prey!

In the darkness I saw a shape. Prey! I saw the bulk, the curved back. I saw the horns. Two very long and a shorter one.

The horns disturbed me. But too late to do anything but attack! Nothing could stop me. Nothing could escape.

The horns turned toward me.

Hmmm.

I dodged left. The horns turned.

Hmmm.

I slowed down. I stopped.

"Shnorf! Shnorf!" the horned creature said.

I saw the others like myself. All were staring at the horned creatures. All had stopped their attack.

<Maybe now they're calmer,> the voice in my head said. <Um, you guys? Those are Triceratops.>

Huh?

<Jake, Ax, Cassie, Marco, get a grip. You are in morph.>

In morph? Me? Marco?

Yaaahhh! My brain snapped back suddenly. Instantly I was me again. Okay, me again in a body that was fourteen thousand pounds' worth of trouble.

But at that exact moment, one of us attacked.

"ROOOOAAAARRR!" A Tyrannosaurus leaped suddenly to the right, jerked its head left, and chomped its humongous jaws down on the arched spine of a Triceratops.

"Rrr-EEEEE, Rrr-EEEEE!" the Triceratops screamed. And then everything went completely insane. The Triceratops staring up at me lunged. Deadly three-foot-long horns were aimed at my belly, propelled by six tons of weight.

I jumped back, inches from being gored.

Another Big Rex — I don't know if it was Jake or Cassie or Ax — went roaring into battle. The massive jaw tried to clamp on one horn and hold it.

The battle was on. Tyrannosaurus versus Triceratops. The battle every kid with toy dinosaurs imagines. It was sheer, screaming madness.

<You idiots!> Rachel roared. <Back away! Back away!>

But then she and Tobias joined the fray, trying to help. They were tiny, but they could attack the lumbering elephant-sized Triceratops with more agility than we could.

My own opponent shnorf-shnorfed a couple of times, then came after me again. I backed away. I didn't need this fight.

<Aaaahhh!> I tripped, staggered back on one knee, and began to fall over. I reached to use my hands, but they were useless. I hit the dirt on my side.

The Triceratops was on me!

<Aaarrrgghhh!> Three feet of horn rammed into me. It caught between two ribs. The pain was shocking and immediate.

But now the Triceratops was vulnerable. Its dangerous horns were stuck, and its front leg was in reach. I opened my jaw, jerked my huge head forward, and clamped down with all my might.

The Triceratops backed away. I released his leg and snapped at his side and missed. He lunged again. I was still down, still on my side, bleeding. I swung my legs forward and shoved my taloned feet in his face. I caught the closest horn between my toes and shoved back with all my might.

I went scooting backward under the impact of

the Triceratops's charge, but those horns didn't get me. Not this time.

I rolled into something that splintered and crashed. A tree! I had just knocked over a tree. I scrambled up, not an easy thing to do when you're a Tyrannosaurus. I got to my feet just as the Triceratops charged again. I backed away, but now there were trees all around me, hemming me in like a cage.

Then, in the darkness, the shocking sight of another Big Rex. It leaped on my Triceratops! It opened its mouth wide, and then sank three dozen or more seven-inch-long teeth into the Triceratops's neck.

"HoooRRROOOOAAARRR!"

"Rrrr-EEEEEEE! Rrrr-EEEEEEE!"

In fury and rage, the big predator yanked the front of the Triceratops up off the ground. An animal the size of an elephant, simply yanked up off the ground.

The Tyrannosaurus shook its head, shaking the screaming Triceratops like a dog worrying a bone.

And then, the Triceratops stopped making sounds. It hung limp. The Tyrannosaurus dropped it and stood over the fallen creature.

"Huh-huh-huh-RRRRRROOOOOAAAARRR!" it bellowed in triumph. The sound shook the leaves in the trees. It rattled through my wounded belly.

"Huh-huh-huh-RRRRRROOOOOAAAARRR!" it screamed again.

It was all the violence of nature, all the ruthlessness of the survival of the fittest, all the power of muscle and bone and claw and tooth, all the ageless, never-ending lust for conquest wrapped into one awesome roar.

I braced myself, afraid it might attack me next.

<Jake? Is that you?> I asked.

<No,> a thought-speak voice replied.

CHAPTER 14

Jake

Cassie stood roaring over the fallen Triceratops. She was the only one still caught up in the Tyrannosaurus's mind. It scared me. It scared me for her. She hadn't wanted to do this morph. And now it had seized control of her. Gentle Cassie was trapped in the mind of a killer.

She swung her head around and glared at me, eyes mad with rage.

<What do we do?> Rachel demanded.

She was scared, too. It scared me all over again, knowing that Rachel was scared. Rachel doesn't scare easily.

<Cassie!> Marco yelled. <Snap out of it!>

Cassie hunched over the Triceratops and began chowing down. It was an unbelievably gross scene. The sun was just coming up, and there in the pink glow, a creature as tall as a tree was devouring a creature the size of an elephant.

I took a step forward on my massive clawed feet.

Cassie spun her head around and bellowed a threat: <Stay away. It's *mine*!>

<Jake, you have to stay back,> Tobias said. <You are invading her territory. That's her prey. She'll have no choice but to defend it. She'll annihilate you.>

<No. She might annihilate this Tyrannosaurus morph,> I said. <But she would never hurt *me*.>

I knew what I had to do. I began to demorph.

<Prince Jake! That is foolish! You will look like another prey animal to her!>

<No. She won't hurt me. She'll recognize me.> I was shrinking already.

<Jake, look,> Marco said, <you may be exaggerating your charm, you know? And if she goes for you, that means we have to try and stop her.>

I hesitated. Marco was right. What if Cassie attacked? But I continued demorphing, shrinking, growing smaller and weaker all the time. The three tyrannosaurs loomed larger and larger above me. They looked to me like Tobias must look to a mouse. Even the Triceratops seemed as vast as a beached whale.

Cassie watched me, curious. Her forward-looking yellow eyes glanced at me, then at her kill, then belligerently at the other dinosaurs.

And then, slowly, slowly, as my own flesh emerged, as my hands grew human fingers, as my face flattened and hair grew and toes replaced claws, she blinked.

<Oh, my God. What have I done?> she asked. She backed away from the Triceratops.

"It's okay, Cassie," I said. "It was just a dinosaur." It was all I could think of to say. I knew it wouldn't help. You can't say "just" an animal to Cassie.

<You got caught up in the morph,> Rachel said. <It happens. All four of you did it.>

<Oh my God!> Cassie cried in horror.

<Cassie, look, it's not your fault,> Rachel said. <It was the Tyrannosaurus. It was just being itself, you know?>

<I told you guys I didn't want to do this morph!> Cassie yelled. She began demorphing. But at the same time, I was returning to the Tyrannosaurus morph.

"Cassie, you have to stay in morph," I said. "We have a mission."

<No! I don't have to be this . . . this . . . killer!>

<Yes, you do, because we need to go kick some butt on these space ants, all right?> Marco said.

<Cassie, come on,> Rachel said. <We need you.>

<I destroyed a living creature. A fantastic living creature,> Cassie mourned.

<Cassie, get over it. This is the late Cretaceous, according to Bird-boy here,> Marco said coldly. <There are no humans. No human civilization. No human morality or religion or philosophy. This is hardcore nature. We're down to survival, here. *Survival*. That's all that counts.>

<Surviving and getting home,> Rachel amended.

<There *are* humans here,> Cassie said. <Us. We *are* human civilization. We have all that stuff inside us. It doesn't matter what year it is.>

<Okay, you're right,> Marco snapped. <It doesn't matter. If this were 1998 or 2000 or 2121, it would still come down to surviving. And when it's down to kill or be killed, all that morality and guilt and all is crap.>

Cassie stopped morphing. For a while no one said anything. Then, at last, Cassie said, <You know something, Marco? You're my friend. I'd do almost anything for you. But you're wrong. Yeah, we're just animals ourselves. But we're the animals who can think. We're the animals who can imagine something better than kill or be killed. I don't think predators are immoral. I'm not an idiot, whatever you may think. But I'm a human,

okay? And I have to think and care, and I have to feel things. Otherwise I might as well be some gangbanger, or a Nazi or, or —>

<A Yeerk,> Ax supplied.

I had finished morphing back to Tyrannosaurus. I waited for Marco to toss out some clever comeback. It never came. Instead, as we once again headed for the Nesk camp, I heard him whisper so that no one but me could hear:

<You know, Jake? I see why you like that girl.>

CHAPTER 15
Ax

The sun had fully risen by the time we arrived at the Nesk base. It was near the lowest slopes of the volcano at a place where a rushing stream came down through the pockmarked gray rocks and gave rise to sparse vegetation.

It was very obviously a military base, not like the peaceful agricultural town the Mercora had built. There were perimeter defenses in the form of robot towers thirty feet tall. The towers bristled with several different types of energy weapons. I could see that widely differing technologies were in use. Obviously the Mercora were correct: The Nesk were scavengers. They had stolen these weapons from a variety of races.

The same was true of the spacecraft parked

within the camp. There were two of the small pyramidal ships Rachel and Tobias had described. But there was also a ship in the more classic airfoil design, as well as very odd oval-shaped craft.

There was little obvious activity within the camp. But then, the Nesk are a strange race. Essentially social insects with the ability to unite and cooperate to a stunning degree. The "bodies" they formed were only assembled in order to operate the weapons and ships they had stolen. The rest of the time, I assumed, they remained as insects.

<Okay, everybody keep moving forward. Casual. Like we're all out for a nice morning walk. Ax, what do you make of it?> Prince Jake asked.

<I think the Mercora were correct and the Nesk have no interest in dinosaurs,> I said. <Those two creatures over there may have walked right through the base, judging by their present location.>

<Iguanodons,> Tobias said.

<Do you see the mound?> Cassie asked. <Looks like a dirt pile, except it's so tall and narrow? That may be their mound. Like a termite mound. That's where their queen will be.>

I had seen the mound. But I hadn't paid it any attention. Now I looked closer. <The mound is defended. Motion detectors tied to what are

probably stun weapons. Dinosaurs may travel freely through the base, but the Nesk protect their mound.>

<So where do we find these alleged nukes?> Rachel asked impatiently.

<Warehouses or storage rooms over there,> Marco said. <Three of them in a row. If it were me, I'd put my most valuable stuff in the middle one. It's more protected. On the other hand, I don't see any guards.>

<I agree,> I said. <But there are probably thousands of guards. Remember, the Nesk will only assemble into a larger creature if they have to hold weapons. But the individual insects are everywhere throughout the camp.>

<Okay,> Prince Jake said. <Here's what we do. Ax and Rachel, head straight for the center warehouse. Ax to point out a nuke, Rachel to grab it, because those Deinonychus hands work better than the Big Rex's. Marco and Tobias flank to the left. Me and Cassie to the right. We rip open that storeroom, get what we came for, and head for the trees over there.>

I felt nervous. Not about possible battle. Well, yes, about that, too. But mostly, I felt nervous about identifying the "nuke." Explosive weapons come in thousands of different shapes and sizes. Some are as big as human automobiles, most are much smaller. Andalite explosive weapons are usually no bigger than a human baseball.

<Ready?> Prince Jake asked.

<Been ready,> Rachel grumbled.

<Okay, everyone just keep moving like we're dinosaurs.>

<Which, thanks to the fact that our lives are totally, completely INSANE, we actually *are*,> Marco said. <I mean, does anyone else think it's just plain weird that we're dinosaurs, getting ready to steal a nuclear weapon from a bunch of antlike aliens, sixty-five million years before the first human being ever said, "Hey, I know what, let's try *cooking* the meat this time?" Does anyone else find this slightly nuts?>

<Nope,> Rachel said.

We advanced on the base, not exactly stealthily. There was a definite impact sound each time my Tyrannosaurus foot hit the ground.

I focused on the center storeroom. I glanced over to the trees. The Nesk ships would have a hard time following us through the trees. But getting to them would be difficult. Especially if it took me a while to find what we were after.

The base seemed empty, deserted. But when I focused my Tyrannosaurus eyes, I could see narrow columns of the antlike creatures spreading out like a web across the entire area. When I lowered my foot near one of the columns, it simply swerved aside.

We passed closer to the small, oval ship. It was perhaps twice the size of an Andalite fighter, but it was made up of three interlocking oval tubes. I wished I had time to study it.

The storeroom, just ahead. It had appeared to be built of crude metal. But when I got closer, I could see that it was actually dirt. It had been built in just the same way as the mound, by the labor of millions of the tiny creatures. Then, it had been covered in some sort of residue and polished till it was bright.

<A bizarre race, these Nesk,> I said. <They have stolen and made use of amazingly sophisticated technology. Yet at the same time —>

Scrr-EEEEEE-eeeee-EEEEEE-eeee-eeee. Scrr-EEEEE-eeeee-EEEEE-eeee-eeee!

A screaming siren! Flashing lights! The robot defense towers blazed with green and blue light. The spacecraft began to power up.

The entire base was suddenly very alive. Very, dangerously, alive!

<A thought-speak detector!> I cried. <They know the Mercora use thought-speak and they have a thought-speak detector!>

<What, are you kidding?> Marco demanded. <How is that possible?>

<Actually, our own Andalite scientists have been trying for years to develop such a system. It would work on the principle of —>

Scrr-EEEEEE-eeeee-EEEEEE-eeee-eeee. Scrr-EEEEE-eeeee-EEEEE-eeee-eeee!

<Here they come!> Cassie yelled. <From the mound! Here they come!>

A red-black river of Nesk poured from the mound. More belched up from the ground beneath us. The soil was alive with them! Millions, millions of them.

<Let's do this!> Rachel cried.

I leaped toward the warehouse. I kicked with my powerful Tyrannosaurus leg and knocked a small hole in the walls. I kicked again. The hole grew only slightly.

<Marco! Go help Ax!> Prince Jake said.

Soon there were two tyrannosaurs attacking the mud wall.

<This is so Godzilla!> Marco said with a giddy laugh. <After this, we head for Tokyo!>

Suddenly, the wall collapsed. I was inside. But I was too tall! My head emerged above the roof of the building. I would have to crumble the roof, too. And each chunk of roof that fell hid more of the things inside the storeroom.

Rachel vaulted past me and began to dig through boxes and crates, the stolen remnants of a dozen alien civilizations. She used her claws to rip them open, scattering their contents, even as chunks of the roof fell on her.

<The ships are starting to get off the ground!> Tobias yelled.

<Prince Jake,> I said urgently. <You can attack the ships more easily *before* they get in the air!>

<Yeah, I thought of that,> he said grimly. <Ax, you and Rachel stay on it, man. Everyone else, let's see just how much damage these dinos can do.>

CHAPTER 16
Tobias

One minute we were standing in a ghost town. The next minute it was like being trapped in the middle of an out-of-control video arcade. Lights! Sirens! Spaceships powering up. The robot security towers shining broad-spectrum floodlights everywhere.

And worst of all, millions of Nesk everywhere! But they hadn't attacked us.

<They haven't figured out it's us,> I said. <They don't know where the thought-speak is coming from. They haven't figured out it's coming from us.>

<They will, soon enough,> Rachel said. <Ax and I are ripping their building apart. They'll figure it out.>

<That weird oval-looking ship is powering up fastest,> Jake said. <Let's get it.>

Three huge tyrannosaurs began stomping toward the ship. I ran ahead of them, faster and more agile in my Deinonychus morph. There wasn't much I could do to damage the ship. Except . . .

I leaped, landed on the outer oval, just as the ship began to rise from the ground.

Crunch!

My weight tipped the ship sideways, slamming the outer ring down into the dirt. And then . . .

WHAMMM!

It was like having someone drop a house on the other end of your seesaw.

I flew through the air, cartwheeled, landed on my dinosaur butt and rolled to my feet.

Cassie had mimicked me. Only when she leaped, she leaped in a much, much larger way. Her massive tonnage ripped open the steel hull, crumpled it like aluminum foil, and flattened a segment of it in the dirt.

<Cool,> she said. <See? I don't mind stomping machines. Are you okay, Tobias?>

<Well, my dignity is hurt,> I said. <That pyramid-looking ship over there!>

We turned and raced toward the second ship.

<Found one!> Ax yelled suddenly. <I don't

know the yield, but it's definitely an explosive device!>

<Then haul butt!> Jake cried. <Rachel, can you carry it?>

<Already have it!>

<Do we take out the pyramid ship or run?> Cassie asked.

<Ax and Rachel, get that nuke outta here, the rest of us will stay and do some more damage. Maybe make it harder for them to come after us.>

I ran for the pyramid-shaped fighter. But the Nesk had figured out what was happening. They'd made the mental breakthrough: It was the dinosaurs who'd become their enemy.

Once they figured that out, the Nesk got nasty.

TSAAAAPPPPPPPP!

A bolt of energy from the nearest robot tower blew a hole in the ground, right where I'd been standing a split second earlier. I felt a jolt of pain. The back half of my left foot was burned off!

I staggered on, but now the pyramid fighter was turning toward us, bringing its weapons to bear.

I ran full at it, but the wound slowed me down. Jake passed me and bounded through the air, tons of muscle and bone becoming one big projectile. He hit the pyramid fighter just as the fighter fired.

CH-CH-CH — !

WHUMPF!

The fighter went rocketing sideways, out of control. And at that moment a second robot tower fired.

TSAAAPPPPPP!

KUH-BLOOOOOOOM!

The energy weapon hit the fighter. It exploded, becoming a small sun of brilliant orange and yellow light.

The impact hit me in the side. I was in the dirt before I knew what had happened. Up I jumped, but my leg was weak as the first injury drained its strength away.

Stinging! The Nesk were all over me, biting, stinging, attacking in the most primitive way.

It was really bizarre. The Nesk were frying everything in sight with highly advanced energy weapons, and at the same time, biting.

<Okay, that's it! Head for the trees!> Jake yelled.

He didn't have to tell me twice. I saw the tree line, illuminated by early dawn light and the brilliant explosions, and I moved out. Pain or no pain, I was running for cover.

But then, my injured leg just stopped working. I was down! Two gigantic tyrannosaurs lumbered by overhead. I should cry out, tell them. But if I did, they'd die trying to save me.

Like some foul-breathed savior, there came a massive, square head. Down it came, jaws open. The jaws closed gently around me. Seven-inch teeth cut into my skin, but did not penetrate muscle.

The Tyrannosaurus lifted me up and up and up. It jolted away. Each step shot pain through my body. But at least I was up off the ground, away from the Nesk.

<Let me know if I bite too hard,> Cassie said. CH-CH-CH-CHEEEEW!

The ground beside me erupted. Cassie was carrying me so that I was looking back. I saw the second pyramid fighter rise up and open fire. Behind it came the other undamaged fighter.

I twisted my head forward. A long, long way to the trees. And between us and the trees, one of the deadly robot towers.

Cassie ran.

The fighters came after us.

No way. No way to make it.

<I'm going to contact the Mercora,> Ax said.

I barely had time to think *what?* when the tower opened fire. The others were all past the tower. But Cassie and I were trapped between the deadly fire from the tower and the advancing fighters.

<This doesn't look good,> I said.

<No. It doesn't.>

Suddenly, Jake and Marco turned back. They came running at the tower from behind. The tower was thirty or forty feet tall. The two tyrannosaurs slammed into a corner of its support beams.

CRRR-UNCH!

The tower did not fall. But it did shake. And it sagged to one side. Just enough that their next shot went wild.

Jake and Marco slammed it again, and now Cassie and I were caught up with them. Cassie gave the supports a devastating kick.

Slowly, slowly, then faster and faster, the robot tower began to fall.

It fell like a redwood, straight down toward the Nesk mound.

It helped, but not enough. We'd been too slow. As we raced for the woods, the fighters closed in. There was no way to outrun them. No way to outmaneuver them. They had us cold.

We were all going to die, sixty-five million years before any of us would be born.

CHAPTER 17
Rachel

We hit the tree line, me and Ax. In my front claws I held a small, oblong white tube. According to Ax, a nuclear explosive.

Let me just say this. Carrying around a nuclear weapon? That'll make you nervous.

I looked back. And I saw what was about to happen.

Three very big Rexes — Jake, Marco, and Cassie — were running. Head forward, tail back, running like roadrunners. A Deinonychus was in the mouth of one Tyrannosaurus. And two spacecraft were practically above them.

It would be point-blank slaughter now.

<The situation is hopeless,> Ax said.

<What do you mean, *hopeless*?> I demanded.

<I am speaking with the Mercora,> he explained.

I remembered him saying something earlier about that. But it was irrelevant to me.

<I'm going back for them,> I said.

<Don't be foolish, Rachel. All you would do is give the Nesk another target.>

<Exactly,> I agreed grimly. <Maybe if they're shooting at me, one of the others will get away.>

I started back out into the open. I heard Ax come lumbering behind me.

CH-CH-CH-CHEEEEW!

The pyramid ship fired.

<Aaaaahhhhhh!> Jake cried.

He fell forward, half a dinosaur.

<DEMORPH!> I screamed.

The pyramid ship turned at a leisurely pace, hovering directly above the writhing, thrashing, helpless monster who was Jake.

CH-CH-CH-CHEEEW!

At point-blank range, the Nesk pyramid ship fired.

<Nooooo!> Cassie screamed.

The blast was blinding. But when the flash cleared, Jake was still there! An electric glow illuminated a sort of invisible shell around him.

<Force field!> Ax said. <The Mercora!>

Then we saw the two Mercora ships. Exactly

like flying saucers. One was just above the pyramid ship. It had projected the force field to protect Jake.

The Nesk pyramid fighter saw it now, too. It fired. At the same instant, the Mercora fired.

BOO-BOOOOM!

The twin explosions were almost simultaneous. The pyramid ship and the Mercora saucer both blew apart. I thought I saw a big Mercora claw go spinning away into the darkness.

The remaining Mercora saucer hovered above Jake and the others. The remaining Nesk ship seemed to hesitate. And while it did, Jake and the others began to demorph.

<They're going to try and take us all aboard,> Ax said. <We should demorph. They don't have room for these bodies.>

I began to demorph, but it was an agonizing wait while the Nesk considered whether to attack or retreat.

The saucer hovered. The Nesk hovered. Standoff.

Jake, Cassie, Marco, and Tobias all demorphed. Ax and I stepped out from the trees, out in plain view. The Nesk were looking at humans for only the second time, and they were seeing an Andalite for the first time ever.

"What do you think they're going to make of you?" I asked Ax.

<Perhaps they will think that the Mercora have acquired powerful new allies,> Ax said.

As if the Nesk had heard him, their ship suddenly veered off and retreated to the wreckage of the base.

I laughed. "Guess you're right, Ax. Looks like the Nesk have had enough. Modern age or Cretaceous, no one can beat the team of human and Andalite."

The Mercora saucer picked us up, us and our little nuke. But they were a grim, depressed bunch of aliens. It was hard to tell at first. But then I noticed that each of them was minus one of their smaller legs. There were just oozing stumps.

"What happened to your legs?" I asked. But even as the words were out of my mouth, I saw the limbs in the corner. They were laid out on a brightly colored cloth which was draped over a shelf. There was something ceremonial about it. Almost religious.

<Can you explain the meaning of this?> Ax asked politely.

<We must make the sacrifice of pain. The legs will regenerate, but those we honor will not,> the Mercora pilot said. <This is a symbol. It speaks to our spirit's pain, by echoing it in physical pain.>

"They did this for the Mercora who were in the other ship?" Jake asked.

<For those who were in *both* ships,> the pilot said. <To be killed is a sadness. To kill is a sin.>

"You'd fit right in with these guys, Cassie," Marco said.

Cassie ignored him. "Our legs and arms do not regenerate," she said to the Mercora.

The pilot responded, <Then you must bear the pain inside.>

"Yes," Cassie said. "I will."

"Thanks for saving us. We're sorry about the Mercora on that other ship," Jake said. "We owe you. We owe you big. I don't know if that concept means anything to you, but we owe you."

"That goes for all of us," I added. "Anything we can ever do for you . . . I mean, until we get back to our own time. *Any*thing."

<Don't make promises you can't keep, Rachel,> Tobias said in a thought-speak whisper only I could hear. <It will only make it worse later.>

I looked at him for an explanation. But the eyes of a hawk give nothing away.

CHAPTER 18
Tobias

Flying beneath the force field was a strange experience. Plenty of heat radiated up from the Mercora town and the fields around it, so there were stunning thermals. But the force field created a sort of glass ceiling above me that I could not hit without risking another busted wing.

A weird experience. But it was good to be flying again. And I felt like I had a sort of mission. I felt someone should see this Mercora settlement. Someone should see all that would be lost, and remember.

It was amazing, really. The universe had so many secrets. Who would have guessed that so long before the humans and the Andalites and Yeerks would even appear on the screen to play out their own life-and-death struggle, there had been an earlier war for Earth?

Through the slight distortion of the force field I could see the Pteranodons in their cliff-side nests. I wondered how they hunted and what they caught in this strange situation. But who could tell? Like all living things, they were doing their best to adapt. They were looking to eat without being eaten. Same as my life as a hawk. The same old cycle: Life trying to stay alive by any means it could find. Life trying to survive the enemies of disease, hunger, fire, flood, and all the animals who were bigger and badder.

I felt the warm wind fill my wings. I turned and circled upward till I could see the entire valley and feel the force field just inches above me. Somehow the Mercora had figured out how to let the rising air pass through the field. They were a smart, advanced, and decent race. I hoped somewhere out in the galaxy there were other Mercora colonies.

Down below, down on what could almost be a street, I saw my friends talking to some excited Mercora. I spilled air and began to dive. Sometimes there's nothing more relaxing than a hurtling dive through the air.

I perched on a land vehicle that was parked near the others.

<What's up?> I asked.

"The Nesk are leaving!" Cassie cried happily. "The Mercora say the Nesk have left Earth! Their orbital ships came down and removed everything from the base."

"Looks like the good guys won," Rachel said. "I think the Nesk saw that the Mercora had some new friends, some serious, butt-kicking new friends." She laughed, mocking her own bravado.

<Yeah. Guess so, huh?> I said.

The Mercora celebrated their victory that afternoon and into the evening. They celebrated by plowing up another hundred acres at the edge of the colony and planting seeds.

The others and I went to the rooms they'd set aside for us. We ate the food they'd provided, and rested on the shaped force fields that passed for furniture.

Night fell, and through the window the comet seemed to fill the sky. I perched where I could watch it.

"So okay, now we have to figure out where and when to use this nuke," Jake said.

<The Mercora have agreed to let us use their computers,> Ax said. <With their help, I can probably recreate the theory behind *Sario Rips*, and then come up with an accurate plan.>

Jake nodded. "Good. Great. Take your time, Ax. Do it right."

"Yeah, why rush? We have all the broccoli we could possibly need," Marco said, making a face of utter disgust.

I watched the night deepen. I watched the head of the comet. And then, I saw it: a stab of flame that shot from the side of the bright white comet head. Blue flame, at a right angle to the trajectory of the comet.

I felt my heart skip a beat.

The Mercora noticed it, too. From the streets outside there came a wailing siren.

"What's that?" Marco asked. "Sounds like the cops."

Jake shrugged. "Who knows with the Mercora? They're some strange aliens. Maybe it's Mercora music."

Several minutes later, two Mercora came bursting into the room. Their eyes were fluttering open and shut at an alarming rate. Their two weak-looking hands were waving wildly.

<The Nesk! They cannot accept their defeat. They have decided if they cannot have this planet, then neither can we.>

"What do you mean?" Cassie asked.

<They have diverted the comet. The comet is now on a trajectory for impact on this planet. Here, on this very settlement. In little more than a day, the comet will strike.>

"We can't let that happen!" Cassie said. "You

can't just give up. Isn't there some way you can . . . I don't know, push it the other way?"

The Mercora responded, <Even our most powerful force field could not move the comet. There is only one chance. The explosive device you took from the Nesk . . . We could use our last ship, carry it to the comet and explode the device. It might fragment the comet's head. However . . .>

"They don't want to ask us for the nuke," Jake said.

"That's carrying politeness a long way," Marco said. "If it was me, I'd be like, 'Hand that over, pal.'"

"If we give up the nuke, we have no way home," Rachel pointed out.

"We have no choice!" Cassie said. "Are the six of us more important than this entire settlement? Are we supposed to condemn them to death just because we want to get home again?"

"Wait a minute, are you *serious*?" Marco demanded. "We're gonna give up our only ticket out of here? I don't think so."

"Ax, if that comet hits, how much damage will it do?" Jake asked.

But Ax couldn't answer. He was distracted by what I was telling him in private thought-speak. Distracted by what I was asking him to do.

To the Mercora I said, <Please give us a couple of minutes to consider. Come back then.>

They left. I met Ax's gaze. He was looking at me with his two main eyes. His stalk eyes were staring down at the small but devastating weapon he now held in his hands.

CHAPTER 19
Cassie

The Mercora went away. And when they came back, we gave them the nuke.

I was surprised by the final vote. It was four to two, with Rachel and Marco against. I guess Jake felt he owed his life to the Mercora. Same as I felt. But I was surprised by the quiet way that Tobias and Ax went along. Neither of them said anything. Just voted with Jake and me.

The Mercora took the weapon and raced to their remaining saucer. I watched from the window as it began to power up.

<We need to get out of here,> Tobias said, speaking at last.

"Why?"

<We have to be far, far from here when that comet hits.>

"What do you mean, when it hits?" I demanded. "The Mercora think this will work. They think they can break it up into small chunks that will burn up entering the atmosphere."

Tobias stared at me with his cold hawk eyes. <The nuke won't explode. Ax fixed it so it'll be a dud. And he fixed it so the Mercora won't know till it's too late.>

I just stared. We all did.

"Wait a minute," Marco said. "If we're not using it, we better hope the Mercora can! Hey, genius, we're down here, too! That comet hits and we get pounded five miles down through solid rock. That's gonna hurt."

<No time to explain now,> Tobias said. <Everyone morph to birds. We need to haul out of here in a couple minutes.>

"Tobias, what have you done?" I demanded.

<I did what had to be done, all right?!> Tobias yelled in a blaze of sudden anger. <I did what had to be done. I made the call, so that none of you would have to feel bad about it.>

"You need to explain this right now," Jake said in the low, silky voice he uses when he's really mad.

<Start morphing or I'll explain nothing,> Tobias said. <Just do it!>

113

Rachel started morphing to her eagle morph. Jake hesitated, but there was a force to Tobias I'd never heard before. Jake began to morph. Then Marco. Ax. What could I do? I had to go along. I had to morph.

<It's the Cretaceous Age,> Tobias explained. <Late Cretaceous, the last age of dinosaurs.>

"So?" I demanded while I still had a human mouth.

<So what do you think happened to them all, Cassie? Dinosaurs ruled the earth for a hundred and forty million years. You've all seen how weak and helpless we are in this age. You've seen how the only mammals are tiny rats, small enough to avoid attracting the attention of the big dinosaurs. So how do you think the dinosaurs fell and the mammals rose?>

<They . . . they evolved,> I said.

<Yeah, they evolved. But evolution got a great big helping hand. See, about sixty-five million years ago . . . around now . . . something — they don't know if it was an asteroid or a comet, but *something* — hit Earth. Very hard. Hard enough to fill the atmosphere with dust, block the sun, and bring on a colder climate. And that's how the dinosaurs died.>

<You don't know it's *this* comet!> I cried. <You don't *know*!>

<Yes, I do,> he said. <No one in our time ever

found a Mercora fossil. Which means they never prospered, never populated the planet, never grew beyond this one handful, this one settlement. *This* is the comet. *This* is the time. Today is the end of the Mercora. And today . . . today is the end of the dinosaurs.>

I wanted to tell him he was wrong. But I knew he wasn't. I wanted to cry. But I had become an osprey. Birds don't cry. It was monstrous, horrible.

Inevitable.

<We're going to let these people, these Mercora, we're going to let them die?> I asked.

<I'm surprised you, of all people, don't understand, Cassie,> Tobias said. <It's about more than these Mercora. The entire planet will be changed today. A million species will begin to die. A few weeks or months or maybe years from now, the last Tyrannosaurus is going to die. And because of that, other creatures will begin to evolve. Including . . .>

<Us,> I said. <Homo sapiens. Homo sapiens, who could never have evolved unless the dinosaurs had died out.>

<So that comet *has* to hit,> Rachel said.

<Yes. That comet has to hit,> I said. I hated saying it. I hated thinking that the brave little settlement of Mercora was going to be destroyed. But this was destined to be a day of annihilation,

and I'd known from the start we couldn't change history. All of this had already happened. Sixty-five million years before I was born.

Ax said, <They will have to drop the force field when their ship takes off. We will need to be in the air, ready to slip out.>

He was right. Tobias was right. I knew it. But it made me sick inside. And I wasn't the only one.

<You know, these guys saved us. Saved *me*,> Jake said. <I don't like this, running off like this. Maybe we could warn them. Maybe they could get away, get off the planet.>

<They lack the ships,> Ax said. <Their struggle with the Nesk has left them with only that one ship. Besides, what if they found a way to survive? We would have altered history in a very large way.>

<This stinks,> Jake said bitterly. <I don't run out on people who've saved my life.>

<You have no choice, Jake,> Tobias said.

<The ship is almost ready to launch,> Ax said. He'd been keeping watch with his stalk eyes.

<Now or never,> Tobias said.

<Now,> Marco said.

<Yes,> Ax agreed.

<No choice,> Rachel said, sounding more conflicted than I would have expected.

<Yeah,> Jake said. <It's really not up to us to rewrite history.>

I wanted to laugh. We acted like we were making a decision. But Tobias had already made the hard decision. The comet would not be stopped. The only question now was would we run away and try to live? We knew the answer to that.

<Thanks, Tobias,> I said.

I don't know if he thought I was being sincere or sarcastic. I wasn't sure myself.

I opened my wings and flew.

CHAPTER 20
Jake

We flew. Up through the force field just as the doomed saucer lifted off.

The Mercora were all out to watch the ship take off. The ship that carried all their hopes with it. They didn't see us in the darkness.

I was mad at Tobias. I was mad at Ax for helping him. But I knew they'd done the right thing. My being angry was the proof of that. See, even though I knew Tobias was right, I could get mad at him. I could try and blame him for the tragedy that was about to occur.

Which meant I didn't have to blame myself.

We flew, up and up. It was dark and we swept past so quickly that the Pteranodons didn't even notice us. They were day hunters. Actually, so were we, in our bird-of-prey morphs. Our eyesight was not much better than human in the darkness.

We flew up and out of that valley where the funny crab creatures grew their broccoli. Up into sky untouched by any artificial light, and toward the ocean.

The comet was amazing, and I guess it would have been beautiful. If we hadn't known what it was. If we hadn't known what it meant.

We flew for close to our two-hour time limit. We demorphed, then remorphed as quickly as we could. This time Cassie and Rachel used their owl morphs, so they could guide us all in the darkness.

<How big a boom will this thing make when it hits?> Rachel asked.

<That depends on the speed of the comet and its size,> Ax said. <The Mercora have observed the comet. They say it is approximately five of your miles across. It is approaching at a speed of fifteen miles per second.>

<Per *second?*> Marco asked.

<Yes. When it hits it will release as much energy as, say, a million of the nuclear weapons on that submarine.>

<Excuse me? A million nukes?>

<Well, assuming the "nukes" are reasonably well-made examples of primitive nuclear tech-

nology. I am being very approximate,> Ax said. <There will be shock waves. One shock wave will go forward into and through the earth. It will compress the rock beneath it, which will release all the carbon dioxide trapped there. There will be a huge fireball from the exploding gases and from the vaporized comet itself. Everything within a hundred miles or so, every animal, every plant, everything, will be incinerated. There will be a huge crater, maybe ten, twenty miles deep.

The second shock wave will bounce back from the impact. It will blow massive quantities of burning rock all the way out into space. These burning rocks will fall across a wide area. As they reenter the atmosphere they will probably cause a massive heat wave, so hot that trees and grass will catch fire and burn. Any living thing out in the open will be cooked alive as —>

<Enough!> Cassie cried.

<Yeah. That's probably enough information,> I agreed. <The question is, how do we live through this?>

<And are we sure we want to,> Tobias said darkly. <The next few years on planet Earth will not be fun. First fire, then darkness. Darkness and cold and death everywhere.>

<Look, I'm interested in surviving,> Rachel said. <Period.>

<The shock wave is the first threat, then the

120

intense heat,> Ax said. <When the comet strikes, perhaps we should be in the water.>

<We're better off flying till the last minute,> I said. <We'll make more distance. We follow the coast north, then, at the last minute, we head out to sea.>

We flew. All through that night, only stopping to demorph every two hours. The sun rose over a scene of breathtaking beauty. We were over a river delta. A hundred glistening streams all heading for the ocean. And in that lushness, the dinosaurs. Slow Triceratops, and herds of huge Saltasaurus, the long-necked, long-tailed dinosaurs we'd encountered before. There were hadrosaurs and gigantic crocodiles and Pteranodons diving for fish.

Great, lumbering giants. It was a world where elephants would have seemed only average in size. Hundreds of species of dinosaurs, each a miracle of nature.

And yes, here and there as we flew we saw the tyrannosaurs and the other great predators. For some reason, although Tyrannosaurus had repeatedly tried to kill us, it was the Big Rex I pitied most.

They were so sure of their power. So confident. This was their planet and they were the kings. I wondered if they ever looked up and noticed that something was different in the sky. I wondered if they, too, saw the comet and felt a quiver of fear.

The comet was visible even in the brilliant daylight now. And it was beneath that comet, and above the teeming life of the Cretaceous, that we flew.

We rested at last in the high branches of a tree. All except Ax, who stayed below. Tobias was right at home there in the trees. And we humans could hang on and feel somewhat safe.

Cassie laughed a sad sort of laugh. "Well, here we are, just a few tens of millions of years early. Primates will evolve, and they'll learn to live in the trees, running from the saber-toothed cats and other predators. And here we are now, just a little early."

"By now they know," Rachel said, looking back in the direction we'd come from.

"Who?" Marco asked her.

"The Mercorans. They know the nuke didn't go off. They know it's all over for them."

Marco nodded. "Yeah. I wonder if they know why? I mean, that we did it. I wonder if they've figured out that we didn't come from some far-off place, but from some far-off time on this planet. I wonder if they'll figure out why we . . . you know, *why*."

A Saltasaurus came by and stuck his snake

head up into the tree, indifferent to us, and munched some leaves.

Night came again, and now we flew on urgently, desperate for every last mile. And finally, Ax said it was time.

We veered out to sea. We landed in the water, hoping that we could avoid being eaten in the few minutes that remained. We morphed to dolphin, and waited for the world to end.

CHAPTER 21

Cassie

I stayed on the surface to watch the end.

The comet was a blazing torch as big as a mountain. It hit, and the entire planet shuddered from the impact. You could almost imagine Mother Earth crying out in pain. But you know, Earth is just a big ball of dirt and water and air and life, spinning through space. It's only important because it's ours. The universe didn't care that the orbit of Earth and the trajectory of a comet would intersect at this time and this place.

And yet in my mind, in my heart, I cried out for Earth.

The explosive power of a million nuclear weapons went off all at once. It was as if a giant had swung a hammer the size of the moon into our planet. I felt the impact in my insides.

The explosion seemed to rip the universe apart.

But I never felt the concussion. Because suddenly, I was no longer in the ocean watching the doom of the dinosaurs.

I was floating above it all. Floating in air, but not really. In space, only I could breathe.

<The *Sario Rip*!> I heard Ax cry. <The impact of the comet is collapsing it!>

But this time the travel through time was different. We weren't suddenly back where we started. We were hurtling through a void, hurtling past a videotape set on fast forward.

I saw the crater. It was a hole big enough to lose a dozen cities in. Flaming hot debris exploded outward. A red-hot fireball rolled across the landscape, burning everything, a blowtorch on dry grass.

Trees exploded into flame. Dinosaurs crinkled and blackened and fell dead where they stood, no time even to cry out. The burning wind expanded outward. The sky itself seemed to burn! But then the fireball weakened and from the wreckage rose smoke and dust. Earth was hidden by a blanket of smoke and dust. The sun was blotted out.

Earth began to freeze, and still more creatures died.

It was all passing before my eyes now, faster and faster. The sky cleared as acid rain fell, disintegrating many plants and starving the remaining dinosaurs. The plant-eaters were too few now. The herds were gone. Only a few pitiful remnants were left, then even they were gone.

I saw, in a flash, the last Tyrannosaurus, wandering hungry, thin, weakened and alone, across a blasted landscape. It was looking for the prey that was no longer there. And then it fell.

Time sped up, and the continents floated across the surface of the world. I watched Antarctica slide to the bottom of the planet and grow icy. I watched the Atlantic Ocean appear where only an inland sea had been. India broke away and then slammed violently into the bottom of Asia, rippling up the Himalaya Mountains.

Ice sheets advanced and retreated. Forests spread and withdrew and spread again. Mountains rose up sharp and craggy, then crumbled slowly to softer, smoother shapes.

And everywhere, the small, brown, fur-covered creatures increased in number. They filled the land the way the dinosaurs had. They migrated into the seas. They became plant-eaters and meat-eaters. Big and small, cute and deadly, slow and fast. And suddenly, there they were in

126

the trees, swinging from branch to branch. And an instant later, some were banging rocks together and forming tools of bone and wood.

They walked erect, on two legs. They built huts and villages and cities. But all of this passed in a flash. Because in the long, long history of Earth, the entire history of Homo sapiens is not even the blink of an eye.

The dinosaurs ruled for a hundred and forty million years. Humans have existed for less than one million years.

I was in water again.

My friends were there, too.

I fired my dolphin echolocation clicks and "saw" ships in the water. And I felt the last, dying echoes of the underwater nuclear explosion that had first opened the *Sario Rip*.

<We're right back when we began,> Ax said.

We demorphed near the beach and when we climbed out, there was the boardwalk. It was still raining. There was no volcano. No giant footprints in the sand.

We went to our homes, dazed, awed, and watched the news reports of the terrible disaster at sea. A disaster that, fortunately, had not resulted in any deaths.

The Navy diver who was the hero of the rescue swore she'd been led to the submarine by dolphins. Some people suggested maybe she was suffering from hallucinations brought on by the depth and by breathing the wrong mix in her scuba tanks.

I returned to my life, feeling strange and out of place. That night Jake came over. We went outside.

"I tried morphing the Tyrannosaurus," he said. "Nothing. Didn't work."

"You could ask Ax. He may know why."

Jake laughed. "Yeah, but even if he explains it, I still won't understand it."

"Maybe it was all just a dream," I said.

"No. Not a dream," Jake said. "But it all happened a long time ago."

"Were we always there? I mean, were we meant to be there? To do what we did? Was everything supposed to happen a different way? Should this planet be ruled by the Mercora today? Or the Nesk? Should there still be dinosaurs stomping around? Did we make it all right or mess it all up?"

Jake didn't have an answer, so I slipped my arm through his. We looked up at the sky for a while. "No comet," Jake said.

"Not today, anyway," I said.

A note:

<Hi, it's me, Tobias. After we got back from our adventure in the late Cretaceous, I looked up some of the dinosaurs we encountered: Tyrannosaurus, Deinonychus, Saltasaurus, Spinosaurus, Elasmosaurus, Kronosaurus, and Triceratops. All of them were around during the Cretaceous Age. But paleontologists seem to think some of them, like Spinosaurus, were extinct by the *middle* Cretaceous, whereas we were in the *late* Cretaceous. All I can say is that I was almost eaten by a supposedly extinct Spinosaurus. So who are you going to believe? Me, or a bunch of scientists with some old fossils?>